# He frowned. "Are you sick?"

"Off and on."

"Off and on... What does that mean?"

She watched him steadily. And then his gut tightened. It felt like all the oxygen was being sucked out of the room. The nausea over the last several weeks. The dizziness. The exhaustion... How the hell could he have missed it? How could he have been so oblivious?

All of a sudden, he was the one who felt sick.

"Marley," he said. "Are you..."

She was quiet for a long, meaningful moment. And then she swallowed visibly. "I'm pregnant, Owen."

He leaned back, feeling like she'd just hit him with a baseball bat. With his own baseball bat.

Dear Reader,

As you open the pages of Marley and Owen's story, the days in Christmas Bay will be getting longer, the breeze coming off the ocean, softer and warmer. Summertime is here, and with it, evenings at the minor-league baseball park where Owen will be pitching shutout games and Marley will be in the announcer's box calling them. Nobody will guess that they're trying their hardest not to fall in love, or more, that there will be a surprise baby coming soon.

I hope you'll enjoy this next installment in the Sisters of Christmas Bay series as much as I enjoyed writing it. So, grab an icy drink, find a shady spot and come back to our little town on the coast. I'm so glad you're here!

*Kaylie Newell*

# Their All-Star Summer

---

## KAYLIE NEWELL

# HARLEQUIN®
## SPECIAL EDITION™

ISBN-13: 978-1-335-72471-7

Their All-Star Summer

For questions and comments about the quality of this book, please contact us at CustomerService@Harlequin.com.

Harlequin Enterprises ULC
22 Adelaide St. West, 41st Floor
Toronto, Ontario M5H 4E3, Canada
www.Harlequin.com

Printed in U.S.A.

Recycling programs for this product may not exist in your area.

For **Kaylie Newell**, storytelling is in the blood. Growing up the daughter of two writers, she knew eventually she'd want to follow in their footsteps. She's now the proud author of over twenty books, including the RITA® Award finalists *Christmas at the Graff* and *Tanner's Promise*.

Kaylie lives in Southern Oregon with her husband, two daughters, a blind Doberman and two indifferent cats.

Visit Kaylie at Facebook.com/kaylienewell.

### Books by Kaylie Newell

### Harlequin Special Edition

### *Sisters of Christmas Bay*

*Their Sweet Coastal Reunion*
*Their All-Star Summer*

Visit the Author Profile page
at Harlequin.com for more titles.

For my mom, the most beautiful woman I know.
Thank you for teaching me to love books.

K.

## Chapter One

Marley Carmichael was home.

She couldn't quite believe it as she looked around the small pizza parlor she used to frequent as a teenager, complete with a sizable chip on her shoulder.

Taking a deep breath, she ran her fingers over the rim of her wineglass. She kept thinking of that old cigarette ad—*You've come a long way, baby.* She *had* come a long way. She was an adult now. Twenty-nine in a few weeks and on the verge of starting her dream job, something she'd been working toward her whole life. And that chip? It was nothing but a reminder that she could do hard things. Being back in Christmas Bay was going to be hard. But she could do it. She'd done a lot harder.

"We forgot to make a toast before dinner," Stella

said. "To the new voice of the Tiger Sharks baseball team."

Marley felt some of the tension ease from her shoulders as she looked back at the three women sitting around the table. The only family she'd ever really known.

"I can't believe you picked Mario's for your celebration dinner," Kyla said, leaning forward so they could hear her above the clamor of the restaurant. "I don't think they've changed the carpet in here since high school."

Stella laughed. "I *know* they haven't changed the carpet since high school."

"I like it," Frances said. "It reminds me of the sixties."

"Groovy." Stella smiled and picked up her wineglass, holding it high. "To Marley. Welcome back, honey."

They all raised their glasses and clinked them together. Some kids in the corner had started an arcade game, and the beeps and buzzes sounded comfortingly familiar. The smell of warm bread and cheese, the view of the ocean outside the smudged windows, the worn, colorful carpet that Frances liked so much. It was all bringing her back to where her heart had been the most hopeful. But also the most broken.

"So," Kyla said, setting her glass back down, "how does it feel to be back?"

Kyla probably had a good idea, since her childhood had been similar. Marley and her foster sisters all shared the same kind of baggage, the same kind of pain. It had kept them bonded over the years.

"Honestly, I still can't believe it. I never thought…"

"None of us ever thought," Stella said, putting an arm around Frances. "But here we are."

Frances smiled. Their foster mother was an absolutely beautiful sixty-two, with platinum blond hair and glowing skin. She had kind eyes and a quick smile. She was also struggling with early-onset Alzheimer's—a cold, hard truth that was the reason why Marley had come back to stay. It was the reason they'd all come back to stay.

"I'm just so happy you're here," Frances said. "I might cry."

"Don't do that," Stella said. "Or I'll have to cry with you, and I don't have waterproof mascara on."

"I second that," Kyla said.

Marley took another sip of wine. "I'm happy, too, Frances. And I always wear waterproof mascara, so you just go ahead and cry if you want to."

Across the restaurant, the door opened with a gust of chilly sea air. They all glanced over to see a large group walk in—about five or six women, milling around two men who seemed used to the attention. Marley watched them. The women were dressed up, their hair and makeup done to perfection, while the men looked like they'd just come from the gym. They wore matching Tiger Sharks baseball caps and T-shirts, and were incredibly fit.

These were pro athletes. Marley could tell. She'd

worked around guys like this for years. And the women were groupies. They were too giggly and attentive to be anything but.

"Oh my God," Stella said, twisting around in her seat. "Do you know who that is?"

Kyla's eyes widened. "I do. Marley, it's one of your new coworkers."

Marley looked over at the men again and realized with a sinking feeling that the taller one did look familiar. *Oh, no...* He'd definitely changed, grown. He was bigger now, thicker in the shoulders and chest, but it had been a decade since she'd seen him last. And even though she was a baseball fanatic, she hadn't followed his career because he'd been such an arrogant ass back then. She hadn't really cared what happened to him and his batting average.

"Owen Taylor?" she managed, watching as one of the women slipped her arms around his waist.

"In the flesh," Stella whispered.

Frances frowned. "Who's Owen Taylor?"

They glanced at each other, knowing this was another example of Frances's memory loss, since nearly everyone in Christmas Bay had heard of him at one point or another. He'd been on the brink of superstardom in high school. He and Marley had been in the same grade, and she remembered the night he'd shattered their school's strikeout record like it was yesterday. After that, he'd been pursued by every college scout imaginable and had his pick of full-ride scholarships. She thought he'd ended up somewhere on the West Coast—UCLA, maybe. She didn't know because she'd chosen to block him and his cocky swagger from her mind. She loved baseball. She didn't necessarily love all baseball players.

"The pitcher, Frances," Kyla said.

The kids who'd been playing the arcade game apparently recognized him, because they abandoned it and rushed over. The teenage girl behind the counter looked flushed, batting her eyelashes as he turned his hat around backward and grinned down at her. He was enjoying this. All of it. Some things never changed.

Marley leaned back in her chair and narrowed her eyes at him. "Don't tell me he's playing for the Sharks."

"He's playing for the Sharks," Stella said matter-of-factly.

"He's *my* age."

"Are you saying you're old?"

"No! But he is. For a pitcher in the minors."

"He signed on last season for a two-year contract. The paper wrote an article about it. Frances, you clipped it out, and we were going to send it to Marley before she moved out here, but Beauregard threw up on it, remember?"

Frances looked resigned. "Cats. Thankfully, I don't remember that."

"He washed out in college," Stella said, "because he didn't take it seriously enough or something, and he's been trying to get back on his feet ever since. The

Sharks picked him up, and of course, he's really good. Setting all kinds of minor-league records, making the ladies swoon... Even though he's *old*."

Ignoring her teasing, Marley took a sip of wine. What she really wanted to do was go back to her little town house overlooking the pier, crawl into bed and forget she'd ever seen Owen Taylor again. Being in the same room with him was bringing back all kinds of memories. Memories of her childhood. Memories of being an outsider. Memories of being sad and alone, and having to face a new life in foster care.

"I think it's kind of romantic," Kyla said. "Him never giving up his dreams like that."

Stella gave Marley a knowing look. "You still don't like him, do you?"

"What's to like?"

Just as she said this, he turned to survey the room like he was surveying his kingdom. Marley stiffened as his gaze swept right over them. He was still gorgeous, no doubt about that. With that maddening tilt to his mouth, like he knew exactly what kind of attention he was commanding, and from whom.

"Huh," Kyla said. "There seems to be plenty from where I'm sitting."

"Shush," Stella said. "You're taken."

"Yes, but I'm not dead. I can still look."

"You don't know him," Marley said. "I graduated with him, remember? He's a toad."

"Owen *Taylor*," Frances said, sitting back and

crossing her arms over her bedazzled sweatshirt. Frances bedazzled everything. "I remember him now. Marley, didn't he give you a hard time in high school?"

The truth was, everyone had given her a hard time in high school. She'd been the only girl writing sports copy for the *Pirate Ship*, their school paper. And to make matters worse, she'd had a painfully awkward way about her. It wasn't necessarily a surprise that someone like Owen hadn't been nice to her. Still, when she thought about it, it made her bristle all over again. She remembered a particularly awful day when she'd tripped and fallen in the school parking lot, dropping her books in front of a large group of athletes and upperclassmen. Owen had laughed the loudest, his deep, masculine voice ringing in her ears and egging everyone else on. Never mind that she'd skinned her knees and had tiny bits of gravel embedded in the palms of her hands for a week. But her pride, her heart, had been hurt the most.

"Yes," she said. "Toad."

Stella winked at her. "Wow. You *really* don't like him."

"It's not that I don't like him..." That was a lie. She couldn't stand him. "I'm just indifferent, that's all."

"But you're going to be employed by the same team," Kyla pointed out. "How's that going to be?"

"It'll be absolutely fine, because Marley is a professional, aren't you, honey?" This from Frances, who always had her back.

She smiled. "Thanks, Frances. And honestly, you guys, I'm used to men who think they're God's gift. He's nothing special." Another whopper. There'd always been something special about Owen Taylor. She'd known it when he'd pass her in the hallways or brush by her when she was standing at her locker. She'd known it when he'd step onto the field, underneath those brilliant stadium lights. She'd known it, and so had everyone else.

"Do you think he'll make it to the majors?" Stella asked, setting her napkin on her empty plate.

Marley shrugged. "Who knows? He's talented, but it takes a lot more than talent. If he screwed up that badly in college, it might be hard to shake that reputation. And now he's past his prime…"

"If your late twenties is past your prime," Frances said, "what does that make me? Never mind. I don't want to know."

Kyla laughed and rubbed Frances's back. "It makes you fabulous, Frances. You only get better with age."

"That's not what my wrinkles say."

"What wrinkles? You barely have any." Stella looked at her watch. "And I hate to break up the party, Frances, but we have to be at the shop at dark o'clock in the morning. It's getting pretty late."

Frances sighed. "Inventory. I forgot about that."

"We'll get it done. And with both of us, it might even be fun. Who knows?"

.

Frances looked skeptical but pushed her chair out and stood, reaching for her purse.

Stella stood, too, and looked down at Marley and Kyla. "Ready?"

For some reason that she couldn't quite grasp, Marley didn't want to leave right then. She cleared her throat and smiled. "I still have a little wine left…"

"Me too," Kyla said. "It'd be a shame to waste it."

"Okay, then. Drive safe. Love you."

"Love you, too."

Frances leaned down and gave them both hugs. And then she and Stella were out the door. Marley could see them through the window running for the car through the light evening rain.

With her pulse skipping, she let her gaze shift back to the man across the pizza parlor.

He was leaning against the counter now, the group that had been surrounding him clearing some. He grinned at something someone said, and two long dimples cut into each cheek. His jaw was scruffy, a shade darker than his shaggy blond hair, and his skin was that same sun-kissed golden brown that she remembered so well. Good Lord, he was gorgeous. He'd always been a good-looking boy, but the years had been especially good to Owen, and now he was simply striking.

She shifted in her seat, suddenly aware that Kyla was looking right at her.

Her cheeks burned. "What?"

"Shopping?"

"Uh…"

"I said we should go. I've been wanting to check out that new boutique on Second. They've got the cutest things in the window. Do you want to come with me next week or not?"

"Oh, yes. Sure. That sounds great."

Kyla glanced over her shoulder, then back at Marley with a smile. "You sure do seem distracted."

"I'm not distracted."

"Then what did I say before that?"

"Before what?"

"Before asking you to go shopping?"

Marley tucked her long bangs behind her ears, flustered. Kyla had a way of being able to read her mind. It was hard to hide anything from her, always had been.

"Just that you…that…"

"See? Distracted."

"I'm not."

"Listen, I don't blame you. The man is beautiful. It's hard not to stare."

"Was I staring?"

"You were definitely looking. Like half the people here."

"It's just strange," Marley said. "That I'm back here after all this time. That he's back here. And now we'll be seeing each other every day, and after how it was in high school…"

"You should just go say hello," Kyla said with a shrug. "Nip it in the bud."

"What? No way," she said evenly. Stubbornness. She'd learned it from Frances. "Besides, he probably won't even remember me, and I'm not a glutton for punishment."

"But he might, and then you could start fresh."

Kyla was practical to a fault. And she wasn't wrong. Going to say hello would be the mature thing to do. After all, they were going to be working for the same organization. The thought made her belly twist. How, exactly, had that happened?

Kyla sat up straight and gave her a look. "He's headed this way."

Marley glanced over, and sure enough, he was walking right toward them.

Her toes curled inside her sneakers. No. There was no way he was coming over here. Why would he? What she'd said a minute ago was true—she didn't think for a second that he'd remember her. They hadn't run in the same circles in high school. He'd been popular and outgoing. She'd been the quiet introvert, with that ever-present chip on her shoulder. Nope. He was going to walk right on past, and that was just fine with her.

She looked down at her now-empty wineglass, wishing there was more chardonnay left. Wishing she could summon up some confidence of her own. If being in the same room with Owen Taylor was going to have this kind of effect on her, then what would being employed by the same baseball team do? She was so proud to be making history as the Tiger

Sharks' first female announcer. Thrilled to have broken through that glass ceiling. But she wasn't fooling herself that it'd be easy. She knew she was going to have to prove herself over and over if she wanted to be taken seriously by men like him. She couldn't and wouldn't let his all-American good looks unsettle her. She'd come too far for that.

Forcing herself to look up again, she locked eyes with him as he passed. And he did pass, just like she guessed he would.

But he also gave her a wink and a knowing smile.

And that part was a surprise.

Coming back to Christmas Bay was going to have its perks, Owen could tell. Back here, he was a big fish in a small pond, and that didn't exactly suck. The reception he'd gotten walking into Mario's hadn't sucked, either. In fact, it was only reinforcing what he'd already convinced himself of—that climbing his way back up the baseball ladder was going to be much easier on his home turf.

The rest of the world might think of him as a has-been, and maybe he was. But Christmas Bay was going to give him another chance. He was playing on the farm team for the Mariners, and that was a big damn deal. He just hoped he wouldn't screw it up this time around.

As he walked by the table to his left, he smiled at the pair, enjoying this part. But it was the pretty blonde on the end who caught his eye. She was look-ing steadily back at him without a hint of the appre-ciation he was used to getting from everyone else in his orbit.

He winked, and she visibly stiffened. He realized he knew her then, and something stirred inside his chest. A feeling of guilt, maybe. Of regret. Since he'd been home, he'd run into a lot of people from his past. Mostly from old part-time jobs or from high school. And he'd been a jackass in high school. Espe-cially to awkward, defensive girls like Marley Car-michael. He wasn't proud of it, but he wasn't proud of a lot of things in his life. He'd just go ahead and add that to the list of disappointments he'd racked up over the years.

The door to the men's bathroom swung open just as he was reaching for the handle, and nearly hit him square in the face.

"Oh! Sorry, dude," Max said, stepping out. "I al-most knocked you out."

"It's okay. I wasn't paying attention."

His friend nodded over Owen's shoulder. "Did you see our new announcer is here?"

"Where?"

"Right there. The table by the window. In the gray."

Owen turned to look. "The blonde?"

"I saw her with the VP the other day getting a tour of the park. She's kind of hot, so I asked around. You know."

Owen smiled. He did know. Max was nothing if not consistent. He played outfield for the Tiger Sharks but was much better at chasing dates than fly balls.

"She was with a team in Iowa," Max continued. "But I guess she's from here originally."

"I know. I went to high school with her."

"No kidding?"

"I recognized her when I walked past," Owen said. "Actually, I recognized the go-to-hell look, but whatever."

"Better make friends, bro. Any tension going into this new season is bad juju, and you need all the luck you can get."

"Wow. Thanks for the vote of confidence."

Max shrugged.

Owen turned to her again. The curve of her shoulders, the slight tilt to her chin. He remembered her coming to his games back then, where she'd sit high in the bleachers. She'd written for the school paper, and she'd always carried a ratty notebook under her arm. He remembered her clothes, baggy and nondescript, clothes maybe chosen to make her blend in, but he'd made fun of them anyway. Because that was the kind of idiot he'd been at the time. Mostly, he remembered treating her the way he treated most of the kids who weren't in his group, like she was beneath him. Some days, he hadn't even acknowledged her enough to tease. Instead, he'd dismissed her existence altogether, acting like she was invisible.

The thing was, as he watched her push her chair in, he saw that she wasn't invisible. Her clothes were still underwhelming, but her generous curves sure as hell weren't.

His chest tightened. No, she wasn't invisible at all. And that was going to be a big problem for someone who was supposed to be focusing exclusively on baseball.

## Chapter Two

Marley stood with her fingers hooked on the chain-link fence, and stared out at the empty field. It was immaculate, with its emerald green grass and perfectly manicured dirt surrounding the stark white diamond of home base. The giant Tiger Sharks logo above the scoreboard only seemed to emphasize the sound of the ocean churning a few blocks away. Another reminder that she was home.

The early-April breeze blew her hair in front of her face, and she pushed it back again with a smile. It had been a good day. A really good day. In fact, it had been one for the books. She'd gotten her keys and had a few meetings with her bosses. The season wouldn't officially start for a few weeks, but she felt ready. More than ready with this beautiful ballpark stretched out in front of her now.

"Getting the lay of the land?"

Startling, she turned at the sound of the voice behind her. And there, in worn jeans and a plain white T-shirt, was Owen Taylor. He had a duffel bag slung over one broad shoulder, and his dark blond hair was wet. He'd obviously just come from the showers and was contemplating her with that easy smile that everyone loved so much. He was movie-star handsome, making her heart flutter despite everything. It was annoying.

She cleared her throat. "I am."

He walked toward her, one hand resting casually on the duffel bag and the other hooked in his jeans pocket. He nodded in the direction of the field. "We've got a new maintenance crew this season. The second we step off the mound, they've got it cleaned up again. Doesn't even look like we practiced today."

She glanced over her shoulder at the freshly raked dirt. Other than a few guys emptying garbage cans, she thought she was the last one out of the gates tonight. The ballpark had been so quiet, with the sun going down behind the concession stand and the sky a brilliant cotton-candy pink, that she'd sat down on the bleachers for a while, caught up in the romance of it all.

"They do a great job," she said. "It's beautiful." Then she turned back to him with a thin smile. "Well, have a good night…"

This wasn't really what Kyla had been talking about when she'd said to nip it in the bud. This was more like Marley pretending she'd never seen him before in her life. Which, of course, was the easiest thing to do. Turned out that coming home meant reverting right back to her old habits. Avoiding things that made her uncomfortable. And Owen Taylor's looks were making her more than uncomfortable. They were making her squirm in her shoes.

She stepped around him.

"I know you," he said.

Her stomach dropped. She was counting on him *not* knowing her. And if he did, very sensibly not addressing it, like she'd chosen to do. After all, they both had jobs here. They were going to have a busy season. What was the point of taking some walk down memory lane when there was zero chance of ending up anywhere good? It was just a waste of time. And Marley didn't want to waste any more of her time. She wanted it to count. All of it.

She turned to him again. "You do?" She hoped she looked appropriately confused.

"We went to high school together," he said. "And I think you probably remember, too. You're just acting like you don't."

"Why would I? I'm not..." Oh, good grief. This was ridiculous. She was a grown woman, not some high school freshman blinded by his light.

"I saw you at Mario's the other night," he said,

"but it took me a second to remember your name. I've always been bad with names."

Of course he was. Because he'd always been too self-absorbed to bother with little things like names. He'd called her Marcy their entire freshman year. That was, when he'd bothered to address her by anything at all.

He took a step closer, and she could smell a hint of aftershave now. It was making her heady.

"Nope, I don't…"

He grinned, his teeth flashing even and white. "Yes, you do."

There was no point. He wasn't going to let it go. "Okay. I do."

"See? That wasn't so hard. You don't have to be shy."

She shot him a look. He really was insufferable. "I'm not shy," she said flatly. "I was trying to be polite. I don't actually like you."

There was a second, maybe two, where she felt a little bad about being so blunt. And then she saw that it hadn't had the desired effect. Far from it. He was now leaning against the fence, watching her with that self-assured look on his face. The one that said he wasn't as bothered by any of this as he should've been.

"How can you not like me?" he said. "You don't even know me."

"I know enough."

"How?"

She shrugged.

"Oh," he said slowly. "You mean you *didn't* like me. Before. In high school."

"Whatever. I'm going home now."

"Marley."

She froze in her tracks.

"Marley Carmichael," he said.

She turned, her face hot.

He dug his hand farther into his jeans pocket. They rode low on his hips, revealing a hint of gray boxer shorts and a sliver of muscled abs. "You had a locker a little way down from mine. Across from Johnson's room."

He was right. She'd watched him come out of calculus every day, and then walk right past smelling like a fresh shower. Her stomach dipped at the memory.

"We had English together, too," he said. "You read a poem in front of the class once. About your dad."

She frowned. "Yes. And you and your friends laughed, as I recall."

His expression fell then. The cockiness replaced by something else. "No, I didn't. I wouldn't have laughed at that."

"I was a favorite punch line of yours. You did."

"My friends might've, but I didn't."

"You seem awfully sure about that," she said, looking away. "Not that we can prove it now, anyway. This is dumb."

"Look," he said, pushing off the fence and taking a step toward her. "I know I was a dick in high school. I'm not denying that. But I know I wouldn't have laughed, because I remember that poem. I remember because I had a dad just like yours."

She looked up at him. The evening sun shone bright in her eyes, and she raised a hand to shield them. She wanted to see if he was serious. If he wasn't just blowing smoke or trying to charm her, for whatever reason. This hit too close to home. It was too tender a subject.

"I'm a lot of things now," he said. "But I'm not that kid anymore. And what I'm trying to do, but screwing it up royally, is apologize."

She watched him. His hair was starting to dry, curling in a little at the nape of his corded neck. He was so tall that she had to tilt her head back to see him clearly. With the sun shining behind him, he looked like an angel sent to break her heart. Because that was what Owen Taylor was. A heartbreaker.

"It was a long time ago," she said. "Really. Water under the bridge."

He readjusted the duffel bag over his shoulder, looking for the most part like he didn't believe that.

"It was a long time ago," he said. "But that doesn't make it okay."

She didn't know if she could forgive him so quickly, but it was a starting point.

She gave him a small smile. "Thank you. I didn't

have an easy time in high school. You probably re-member that part."

"If your home life was anything like that poem…" He shrugged. "I get it. Mine was shitty, too."

He'd said his dad had been like hers. But he couldn't know how bad her father really was. How volatile and cruel. He'd told her daily how stupid she was, once even blaming her for her mother's death, an off-the-cuff comment about the stress she'd caused simply by being born that had haunted her for years. All she'd ever wanted was his love; he was the only thing she'd had left in the world. But in the end, he'd abandoned her. It was something she still struggled with, coming home to find him gone. Simply *gone*. And his parting gift? A debilitating fear of being left behind like garbage. Thank God for Frances, or she might not have known any love at all.

She swallowed down the sudden lump in her throat. She didn't talk about that time in her life for a reason. It always reduced her to this—a little girl in a grown woman's body.

"Well," she said, "it's getting late. I should prob-ably go…"

He raised his eyebrows. "Do you really have to go, or are you just trying to run away from me?"

"I kind of want to run away from you."

"At least you're being honest."

She laughed, unable to help it.

"This is going to come out sounding wrong," he said, "because it's not what I mean at all…"

"Uh-oh."

"Are you single?"

She stared up at him.

"I'm not asking you out," he said quickly. "I'm just asking if you want to grab a drink. So I can apologize for real." He rubbed the back of his neck. "Damn. I guess technically that's asking you out."

"Technically."

"So. Are you?"

"My boyfriend and I just broke up." It was true. She and AJ had been having problems, and when she'd decided to come back to Christmas Bay, they'd called it quits for good. She *was* single now, but she most definitely didn't want the complication of getting involved with someone she worked with. That had trouble written all over it.

He could probably tell what she was thinking, if that teasing smile was any indication.

"I promise," he said, holding up both hands in mock surrender. "Just a drink to say I'm sorry. Then you can go right back to ignoring me."

She grazed her bottom lip with her teeth. She could hear Kyla now. *Start fresh…* She guessed it wouldn't hurt to get to know him again. After all, he was trying, and that said a lot. Plus, she desperately wanted to be part of the team. Just one of the guys, and how better to accomplish that than with a drink after work?

"Okay," she said. "*One* drink. Then home."

He winked down at her. The same wink from Mario's the other night. The one that had made her heart skip a beat. And she wondered if she'd just made a huge mistake.

Owen squeezed through the throng of people at the bar, trying to make room for Marley to follow behind. He'd brought her to the Pump House, a local favorite, but maybe they should've gone somewhere else. It was loud and crowded. And she looked incredibly out of place here, among all the fishermen who'd already had way too many by 7:00 p.m.

There was a Mariners game on the big screen behind the bar, and most everyone was looking up at it, the hum of their talking punctuated every now and then by a collective *aww*, or a cheer at a decent play.

A guy jostled him and apologized, then ran right into Marley, nearly spilling his beer down her front.

Owen reached for her hand.

"I'm sorry about this," he said, leaning toward her ear. "I see an empty table over by the window. It'll be quieter over there."

She nodded and let him lead her through the crowd to the other side of the bar.

And he'd been right. It was quieter over here, and

there was even a decent view of the bay if you craned your neck just right.

Turning, he smiled down at her. "Is this all right? Not exactly Mario's with the fancy carpet, but…"

She laughed and sat down. He sat across from her, trying not to stare. She was incredibly beautiful, although he knew she probably wouldn't believe that. She put off an understated vibe, like she was used to covering up her looks. Probably a direct result of being a female working in a male-dominated field. She clearly had to be twice as tough, twice as serious, as the guys.

That seriousness had drawn him to her tonight, when he'd come out of the locker room to see her standing there staring out at the field. Obviously deep in thought, her shoulders curved in such a way that made him think a weight was settled there. He was curious about her, wondered what had brought her back here after all this time. But most of all, he thought she was one of the prettiest women he'd ever seen, and he was a red-blooded male, God help him.

Still, he'd meant what he'd said earlier. This was only a drink, nothing more. He'd spent too much time clawing his way back to baseball to torch it with another dumpster-fire relationship. He'd done that in college, and look where it had gotten him. Getting picked up by the Sharks was a second chance, and one that would demand every bit of his focus. He wasn't going to let himself get distracted. Even by the lovely Marley Carmichael, who was looking at him with those deep green eyes.

He cleared his throat and leaned back in his chair.

A server came over, her silky hair swept up in a bun and an apron tied snug around her waist. She gazed down at Owen, barely giving Marley a second glance.

"What can I get you folks?"

"I'll have a porter, please," he said. "Whatever you have on tap."

"And I'll have a white wine," Marley said. "Thanks."

The server nodded, giving Owen a flirty smile. He was used to this kind of thing. Sure, he liked the attention and didn't mind the occasional free drink. But it could get weird when it was so brazen like this, especially in front of another woman.

"Don't you play for the Tiger Sharks?" she asked, pointing her pen at him.

"I do."

"I'm a *big* fan."

He scraped a hand through his hair, feeling Marley watching from across the table.

"That's great," he said.

"You're pitching again this season?"

"Yup."

"Then I'll have to get some tickets for sure."

He nodded, smiling up at her. Wishing she'd move on to the next table already.

She stood there for another second, then gave a little sigh. "Okay, then. Those drinks will be right up."

Marley watched her go. "Wow. Does that happen every day?"

"Fans, you know."

"I've worked around minor-league baseball players for a long time, and I'm not sure I've ever seen this level of adoration before."

"It's just because it's a small town. No biggie." He was trying his best to downplay it, but she wasn't biting.

"Uh-huh."

He leaned forward, putting his elbows on the table. This close, he could see a tiny mole on the side of her mouth, and his groin tightened.

"I don't want to talk about me," he said. "I want to talk about you."

She raised her eyebrows, clearly not expecting this. "Why?"

"Because I'm interested. What's your story? What brought you back here? To Christmas Bay?"

She swallowed visibly, looking like she was trying to decide how much to tell him. After all, they'd only gone to high school together. He might as well be a stranger to her now, and as curious as he was, he had to respect that.

But after a second, she leaned forward, too. Seeming to relax a little. "I got put into foster care in middle school," she said. "Frances, the woman who raised me, has this little candy shop on Main Street. Coastal Sweets. She's lived here her whole life."

"Ah, I know that place. Amazing peanut brittle."

"Right?"

"Go on."

"After I left for college, we started noticing her memory slipping."

"We?"

"My foster sisters and I. There's three of us."

He nodded, letting this sink in. He'd never known she was a foster kid. But then again, why would he? He hadn't taken the time to talk to her back then.

"It's been getting worse," she said, "so last year we decided to come home to help. She doesn't have any kids of her own. We're it."

"Do you live with her?"

She shook her head. "Stella does, for now. And we hired a housekeeper a few weeks ago—she cooks and does some light cleaning. But mainly she keeps an eye on things when we can't. Frances loves her, but it's still hard having a stranger in the house."

"So, she lives here in town?"

"She does. In this beautiful Victorian above Cape Longing. It's been in her family for generations."

"The yellow one? That place is incredible."

"It really is. It's also huge, and getting to be a lot to take care of. So is the shop. But Stella started working there in December, helping out until we can figure out what to do next. Kyla's a teacher. She moved back from Portland last summer."

He watched her. "So, she needed you, and you all came back." He snapped his fingers. "Just like that."

"Well, it took some planning. But we're pretty close. Frances is basically our mom. We'd do anything for her."

For reasons he didn't want to think too much about, his heart beat heavily at that. He and his family had grown apart years ago. He never talked to his dad. In fact, he wasn't even sure if he knew Owen was playing ball in Christmas Bay.

"She must be so happy," he said, his voice low, "to have you all home again."

"I do think it's helped. Her memory doesn't seem to be deteriorating as fast as it was, which is strange. There's still so much they don't know about Alzheimer's."

The server walked up with their drinks and set them down on little napkins on the table.

"Here you go," she said with a wink. "Let me know if you need anything else."

And then she was gone, weaving expertly through the crowd with her pen tucked behind her ear.

Owen picked up his beer and took a long swallow. It was cold and tangy on his tongue. Refreshing after a long afternoon of practice.

Putting it down again, he watched Marley from across the table. She'd taken a sip of her wine, too, licking it from her lips. The glimpse of her tongue between her teeth was enough to make his pulse quicken.

"So, you're an announcer," he said, wanting to

keep the conversation going so that he wouldn't be tempted to stare. "What do you do in the off-season?"

"I write freelance sports articles for some syndicated papers around the country. It's a great way to be able to call games and make rent at the same time since announcers don't earn a ton, unfortunately. I'm sure you already guessed that."

He knew they *could* make a good living, but not until they'd made it to the big leagues. Even though Marley landing a position with the Tiger Sharks was a big deal locally, it probably wouldn't be reflected in her paycheck. A grim reality of the job.

She smiled, gazing at him from underneath those impossibly thick lashes. "What about you, Owen?"

"What about me?"

"You were right when you said you aren't that kid anymore. The jerk. The one I couldn't stand before."

"Oh, now we're getting down to it. You couldn't stand me, huh?"

She took another sip of wine, and he thought her cheeks might've colored a little. "Sorry. I let that slip."

"It's okay. I'm a big boy. I can take it."

He said this with a twinkle in his eyes that he knew had a way of melting even the chilliest of hearts. But underneath his sudden desire to have her like him was a feeling of genuine shame. Of wanting, or maybe needing, to take his medicine.

"You can be honest, Marley," he said.

To that, she just shrugged. She wouldn't meet his

gaze. It was telling. A lot of time had passed, but there was still pain there. And it unsettled him.

"In high school, the sun rose and set with you," she said, brushing her hand across the tabletop. "I struggled with fitting in. And then I struggled with the fact that I *wanted* to fit in. And you were so... you were so..."

He watched her. "I was so...what?"

"You were so handsome. It made it worse that you weren't very nice."

Had he been *that* bad? But he knew the answer to that. Women had been nothing but entertainment for him for a very long time—convenient ways to pass the time and boost his self-esteem. His father had really done a number on him. Convincing him he was worthless, that his mother had been worthless, too. And that was a bitter seed that he was still trying to pluck out of his heart to this day.

"So, what happened?" she continued. "Why are you being so nice now?"

Sitting back, he sighed. "What happened to me?" he said slowly. "I grew up."

"Well, I like this new you."

"Oh yeah?"

"You're much better than the boy who teased me between classes."

He frowned. He honestly didn't remember a ton of the details. "I'm sorry."

"You didn't break the mold or anything. I got teased by a lot of kids. I was weird. I probably invited it."

"You weren't weird. And you never invite that kind of thing. Either people are assholes, or they're not."

She worried her bottom lip with her teeth for a second. "Thank you for that."

"You were a loner, though. I remember you always being at the games by yourself." He'd had no idea back then that she'd probably loved baseball just as much as he had. After all, she'd grown up to be an announcer.

"If there was a game anywhere within a walkable distance," she said, "I was there. And then I was writing about it later. It was like getting to experience it twice, which made me happy. It was an escape."

He watched her, something stirring inside his chest. Her blond hair hung in soft waves next to her face. She didn't have much makeup on, which made her look younger than she actually was. She wore a brown blouse that was buttoned all the way to her chin. Before he could stop it, he pictured himself undoing those buttons one by one. It'd be like unwrapping a Christmas present. You didn't have to have a great imagination to know Marley Carmichael was probably just as beautiful naked.

Looking away, he took a swallow of his beer. What the hell? He'd promised her this would be just a drink, and he'd meant it. Imagining her naked was not something a nice guy would do. At least, not the kind of guy she now seemed to think he was.

"What's wrong?" she asked.

"Nothing. Nothing's wrong."

"You got quiet all of a sudden."

"Did I?"

"What are you thinking?"

Now, that was a new one. He didn't get asked what he was thinking very often. Maybe never. And just his luck, the second someone was interested in something other than the speed of his fastball, he was contemplating sex.

His neck heated. "Honestly?"

She nodded.

"I was thinking about your clothes." That wasn't a lie. He had been. In theory.

She gave him a funny look. "What about them?"

"I was just picturing you in high school. You didn't really like to stand out…"

"No, you're right. I didn't want to draw attention to myself. My dad…well. You didn't want to make him mad by wearing something wrong, saying something wrong. Anything was an excuse for discipline. I think he actually enjoyed that part. Making me fear him."

She said that last part like she had something bitter in her mouth. Something she wanted to spit out.

He gritted his teeth, not wanting to think too hard about what kinds of things she'd suffered at home. It brought back memories of his own experiences with "discipline." With walking on eggshells around a volatile parent. With trying not to get popped for the things he said or did.

He cleared his throat. "And now?"

She seemed to ponder that. "Now I need to look the part. The professional. It's not so much about blending in anymore, but just wanting to be taken seriously."

"I don't know that you'd ever blend in, but whatever."

She smiled. "That's sweet."

"I'm not that sweet."

"Nobody ever notices me in that way."

He didn't see how that was possible. But he kept his mouth shut to keep from embarrassing himself any more than he already had. She probably thought he was hitting on her, which was a fair assumption.

This drink was a dumb idea. When had he ever been able to separate attraction and actual physical contact? No wonder she downplayed her looks. She probably just wanted to be left alone.

Leaning on the table, she put her chin in her hand. "So, what's your story?" she asked. "What happened after high school?"

"Oh, man. That's not much of a story."

"Tell me."

"In a nutshell...went to college, crashed and burned, lost my scholarship, disappointed my dad. Well, that makes it sound like he had any hope for me in the first place, which, you know, he didn't."

He took a long swallow of his beer, suddenly wishing it was something harder. Talking about his past never ended well. As a general rule, he avoided it altogether, but she'd asked, and he'd had to say something.

She must've noticed the change in his voice, because she put her hands in her lap, looking like she regretted asking.

"I'm sorry," she said. "About your dad."

"It is what it is."

"Do you still have a relationship with him?"

"We never really had a relationship. He was in and out of the picture. But you know how it is with parents. You always want their approval."

She watched him closely. And something in her eyes made him feel like she gave a damn. Maybe she did, and maybe she didn't, but it was the first time he'd mentioned any of this to anyone in a very long time. It made him feel unsettled, vulnerable. And he didn't want to be vulnerable. Even with someone who might understand exactly where he was coming from.

"Anyway," he said, "it's ancient history. Taught me a lot, though. Not everyone should be a father. Sometimes it's better to accept your shortcomings than to force it and make everyone around you miserable."

"Is that how it was for you?" she asked. "Miserable?"

"I lived."

All of a sudden, there was a faint throbbing at his temples. "Hey," he said, wanting to change the subject, "are you going to the party next Saturday? To kick off the new season?"

"Oh. I'm not sure. Maybe."

"Come on. You have to go. You can get to know some of the guys, the coaches. People you won't get a chance to talk to very often since you'll be stuck up there in that box all the damn time."

She laughed. "When you put it that way…"

"Plus, you're part of the team now. Can't get out of the cheesy events."

"Are there a lot of cheesy events?"

"Wait until the Christmas party."

"Well, thanks for warning me. At least I'll be prepared."

"So, you're going, then?"

"If you're going."

His heartbeat slowed. Which probably had everything to do with how pretty she was and how she was looking at him now. Like they were friends.

Owen wasn't great at being a friend. Never had been. He was too selfish, no matter how much Marley thought he'd changed or how much he said he'd grown. He had grown, but had he gotten that much better? He wasn't altogether sure.

But maybe it was time to find out.

## Chapter Three

Marley walked through the little boutique, running her fingertips lightly over the clothes on the hangers. It was sunny outside, warm for spring on the coast, and the sun shone in through the floor-to-ceiling windows in brilliant shards of orange and gold.

"What about this one?" Kyla said, holding up a pale yellow blouse with tiny pearl buttons marching up the front. "It's so cute."

Stella was the champion shopper in the family. But when Kyla got a wild hair, she was a close second. Marley was another story, but she'd promised to come, and hadn't wanted to back out just because shopping usually gave her a headache. Besides, her town house had felt especially empty this afternoon, with nothing but the seagulls outside her sliding glass doors to keep her company. Spending time with Kyla had sounded nice.

She smiled. "I like it. And yellow looks so good on you."

"Depends on the yellow," Kyla said, holding it in front of herself and gazing in the mirror with a critical eye. "Too yellow, and I look like a banana."

Marley laughed and picked up a skirt with delicate embroidery around the hem. "What about this one? I love the detail."

"Me too. I'll try it on." Kyla draped it over her arm and kept looking. "So, how's work going? You haven't said much about it."

"It's going great. Everyone's been really welcoming."

"Oh, that's good. The owner's nephew is in my class, and he came to the Thanksgiving play this year. He seems nice."

"He is nice." Marley's boss in Iowa had been an absolute ass. She couldn't imagine him doing something as sweet as showing up for an elementary school play.

"And you're getting to know the team?"

She took a deep breath, thumbing through the skirts. The boutique smelled perfumy, like a flower garden, reminding her of summers in the old house above Cape Longing. So many flowers, so many hummingbirds and bees. Like a fairy tale for three lonely, unwanted girls. Like a dream come true.

"Yup," she said. "They're actually having a party next weekend. To celebrate the start of the season."

Kyla looked over, her interest piqued. "Are you going?"

"Thinking about it."

"Marley. You *have* to go."

Marley turned to a rack of dresses and ran her hand over the silky fabrics. Her foster sisters had been the only reason she hadn't turned into a hermit in high school. They'd pushed her to be more social, to let more people in. To learn to trust again. It hadn't been easy, but she'd come a long way since then. Being back here, though—she felt those old tendencies trying to worm their way back in.

"I know," she said, "and I probably will. I mean, I *will*. I'm just a little nervous, that's all."

"Of course you are. That's normal. New job, new people. You can't be the only one who's nervous."

She wasn't so sure about that. She immediately thought of Owen sitting across from her the other night and looking like a Greek god in his perfectly fitting T-shirt. He was the picture of confidence, of smooth, sexy charm. He hadn't seemed nervous at all. In fact, he'd seemed so relaxed that it had felt like they'd known each other for years. It was a warm feeling that had stayed with her.

She didn't have many friends these days. She worked too much to have a decent social life. If someone had told her a few weeks ago that Owen would be one of the first friends she'd make after coming back to Christmas Bay, she would've laughed in disbelief. It actually seemed like her old high school nemesis had grown into a decent guy.

She picked up a little black dress—sleeveless, with a nipped-in waist and flared skirt. The kind of thing that belonged in an Audrey Hepburn movie.

"Oh, that's gorgeous," Kyla said, clutching her chest. "And it would look so good on you."

Marley smiled, catching her reflection in one of the mirrors across the room. She had jeans and a sweatshirt on today, pretty much her regulation weekend uniform. Her hair was in a ponytail, and she'd put on a little mascara before she'd left home. Enough to make her look more awake, at least. But all of a sudden, she wondered what it would feel like to go all out. To walk into a room and have people turn to look. To notice her for once. Before she could help it, she wondered what it would be like to have Owen notice her, and her heart squeezed.

"Try it on?" Kyla said, walking up behind her. "For me?"

"I don't know…"

"With that body? Come on."

Marley had never thought too much about her body, except to try and keep it as healthy as possible. After all, she was the most practical person she knew. Her boobs had always been too big, and the bigger they were, the harder it was to find a comfortable bra. And her hips… Well, her hips were pretty much in the same category as her boobs.

But Kyla looked so hopeful standing there next to her that she couldn't say no. She'd try it on, would have trouble zipping it up, and that would be the end of that.

"Okay," she said. "For you."

Owen stood looking out over the sparkling blue-gray ocean, his elbows resting on the balcony railing. He'd been nursing a beer, something light and cold, and that reminded him of college in a good way, but he was thinking of making a beeline for the door anyway. Most of the guys were here with their wives or dates, and he'd been feeling like a damn fish out of water for the last hour.

Swallowing hard, he glanced over his shoulder at all the couples. The catcher, a good friend named Tommy, had his girlfriend on his knee, her arm slung casually around his neck. They were laughing at something, and he leaned in and kissed her throat. Owen didn't normally think too much about things he didn't have, especially if they weren't baseball related. Usually, he couldn't care less. But for some strange reason, standing there with the sun on his shoulders, he felt especially alone. It was an odd sensation, and one that made his heart feel heavy and tight.

For him, when it came to relationships, the kind

that actually might come to mean something, he'd simply never let himself go there. Why would he? He was his father's son. He had his father's blood running through his veins—someone who'd been cold and mean, and at the end of the day, had split when things got hard. Owen didn't want to be that kind of person. He didn't want to be that kind of man. So, it was just easier to avoid loving people altogether. And that was exactly what he did. He avoided, he dodged, he was an expert at moving on and not getting attached to anyone or anything. It was his superpower.

He sighed, running a hand through his hair. Where had all this come from, anyway? It was too nice a day to be brooding about this stuff. Marley hadn't shown up, and maybe that was a good thing. The way he was feeling now, he didn't know if he could trust himself if she walked through the door.

Draining the last of his beer, he pushed off the balcony and tossed the empty bottle in the recycling bin by the hot tub. He looked around. This was his coach's place—a nice cottage right on the beach. Someday, he wanted something just like it. Only, without all the kids running around everywhere. Four. Coach had *four* kids. Too many, as far as Owen was concerned, but he had to admit, they were pretty cute. He gazed down at the youngest one now, who'd appeared out of nowhere to tug on his pants leg.

"Where's my mommy?"

She looked like she was about to cry. She couldn't be more than four or five, and her chin trembled slightly as she clutched a half-eaten hot dog in one chubby hand. It looked a little worse for wear.

He knelt down to one knee. "I don't know where your mommy is, honey, but I think your dad is in the kitchen."

"Michael took my Barbie, and he won't give her back."

He assumed Michael was one of her brothers. She had three of them, but he couldn't keep them straight. They all looked alike.

"Oh," he said. "Well…" He reached into his back pocket and fished out his wallet. Then he handed her a one-dollar bill. "Tell him you'll trade for this."

Her blue eyes widened. "Money?"

"Just a dollar. But I bet it'll work."

She grinned, and a dimple appeared in one cheek. She looked like she belonged in a Happy Meal commercial. "Thanks!"

She ran off, clutching the hot dog in one hand and the dollar bill in the other.

He smiled, watching her go.

"Um…did you just give my daughter cash for a bribe?"

He looked up to see his coach standing over him wearing a disapproving expression. But honestly, Owen barely noticed. Because Marley was standing there, too. In a black dress that took the air right out of his lungs. Sleeveless and made out of some kind of delicate fabric that shimmered slightly in the sunlight. The effect against her creamy white skin was devastating.

"I..."

"Don't answer that, Taylor," his coach said wearily. "Marley just got here, and I wanted to introduce her to everyone, but Sarah is having some kind of crisis with the dessert. Can you do the honors?"

He stood up slowly, unable to take his eyes off her. "Sure. I'd be happy to."

"Good." His coach turned to her, his short gray hair blowing in the breeze. "I'm glad you came," he said. "The Tiger Sharks are proud to have you."

"I'm glad to be here, too, Coach," she said.

"I'll just leave you kids to it, then." With a fatherly nod, he headed back inside, presumably toward the dessert crisis.

Marley's smoky gaze settled back on Owen. She looked stunning tonight. Smelled even better. He couldn't believe this was the same woman he'd taken to the Pump House—the one in the conservative blouse with all the buttons.

She touched her hair self-consciously. "What?"

"You just look different."

"Uh-oh. Is that good or bad?"

"It's good. It's very good. Not that you weren't beautiful before."

She smiled slowly, her lips glistening pink. "I just

thought I'd experiment," she said. "Try something new. Plus, I went shopping with Kyla, and she has a way of talking me into things..."

He looked down to where the dress hugged her waist, then flared out around her legs. She reminded him of a contemporary Jackie O. Only with blond hair and eyes so gorgeous, they were giving the ocean behind her a run for its money.

"Now that I'm here, though," she said, glancing around, "I feel like it's a little much."

"It's just right."

She looked back at him, and her cheeks were definitely flushed. He couldn't decide if she looked like she wanted to bolt for the door or not. He needed to get her relaxed, talking to people. Or she really might leave, and she was the best thing that had happened to him all day.

"Do you feel like introductions now?" he asked. "Or we can grab a couple of chairs, hang out until you're ready?"

"No, I'm ready. Ready as I'll ever be. I'm anxious, though."

"Why?"

But the answer to that was obvious. She was getting all kinds of curious glances. She'd shown up wearing a cocktail dress in a room full of jeans and T-shirts. It was the perfect metaphor for her new job. He could only guess how that felt, but it couldn't be supercomfortable.

"I don't know," she said. "Baseball has come a long way, but it's still a boys' club deep down."

Stepping forward, he touched the small of her back. "You look great. And you've worked your ass off for this position. Everyone is excited that you're here, part of this team. Enjoy it. This is your moment."

She looked up at him, and the tight expression on her face eased a little. "Do you *ever* get nervous? Like, ever?"

"Sure. But what are you gonna do? You either play ball, or you go home."

What he really wanted was to slip his arm around her waist and lead her through the crowd with her tucked close to his body. He wanted to shield her from anything that might make her uneasy or shake her confidence. But he had to remind himself that that kind of thinking was dangerous. Marley Carmichael was a coworker. Nothing more, nothing less. And she didn't need him protecting her from anything, especially the realities of her new job. She had this. Even if she struggled for a minute or two, she really did.

"Let's do this," he said, motioning toward his teammates. "After you."

Marley sat in the passenger's seat of Owen's truck, watching him walk around the front of it in the moonlight.

She licked her lips, which suddenly felt dry. This had all happened so fast that she felt a little light-headed. A little fuzzy. She'd had a glass of wine at the party, and then, before she knew it, she had two. Honestly, she *never* had a second glass of wine. But she'd been jittery tonight and had been sipping on it before she even realized it was in her hand.

It wasn't that she was drunk—far from it. But she hadn't wanted to drive home, either, so she'd asked Owen for a ride. And now here she was. Not at her town house, but at his place.

If someone asked her why, she wasn't sure she'd be able to tell them. Except for the simple fact that she was wildly attracted to Owen Taylor, who, despite having treated her so badly in high school, had recently begged her forgiveness with undeniable feeling. That alone was hard to ignore. Plus, her little black dress experiment had maybe given her a little *too* much confidence.

Sitting here now, watching Owen reach for the door handle, she knew she couldn't blame the wine for this. The effects of that second glass were already starting to wear off. Her light-headedness wasn't because of alcohol. It was because of the man opening her door. And when he'd asked if she wanted to stop by his place for some coffee on the way home, she'd said yes.

She forced an even breath as he took her hand and helped her out of the truck. The thing was, she was tired of calculating every single move and every single consequence in her life. It was like a different woman was walking up to his front door now, her strappy heels clicking on the concrete. A woman who hadn't lost her childhood to an abusive father. Who hadn't grown up much too fast in every single way.

Marley had always been careful because she couldn't afford not to be. She'd had to toe the line, constantly having to prove how responsible she was because she'd known in her heart that everyone expected her to be *that* girl. The one who didn't deserve anything good.

She had felt so good tonight, slipping on her new dress and easing it over hips that she'd always thought were too wide. It had felt empowering. And when she'd walked out onto that deck and Owen Taylor had looked at her like he had, well… It had felt like she was being seen for the first time in her life.

Pulling the sea air deep into her lungs, she waited while he unlocked his front door.

"Oh, God," he said, turning on the light in the foyer. "Can you wait, like, uh…just a second? I wasn't expecting company."

She smiled and looked down at her shoes. "Sure."

"One second. Promise."

He disappeared inside, where she heard the frantic sound of dishes being thrown into the sink and cans chucked into the garbage. Her heart was hammering inside her chest, but every time her conscience tried to intervene with a *What the hell are you doing?* she'd respond with *It's just coffee. Calm down, Marley.*

She was finding that you could deny just about anything, even to yourself, if you tried hard enough.

After a minute, Owen showed back up at the door. He looked frazzled, his usual smooth demeanor a little frayed around the edges. She could hardly believe that she, of all people, would be affecting him like this. She assumed he probably had women over all the time.

"Sorry. It's kind of messy in here."

She stepped past him and looked around. The house was nice, a contemporary ranch that was decorated in cool blues and grays, glass and metal, and it was very much a bachelor's pad. Clothes were draped across the couch, socks and cleats were strewn over the floor. A few Diet Pepsi cans littered the counter and end tables.

Looking over at him, she raised her eyebrows. "Maid's day off?"

"Something like that." His face colored as he swiped a few T-shirts off the couch and bent to pick up his cleats. "Have a seat if you can find one. I'll make that coffee."

He headed into the kitchen, and she smiled, unable to help it. She thought about him giving the coach's daughter money to get her Barbie back. Owen was such a kid. Pushing his thirties and drop-dead gorgeous, but definitely still a kid. She couldn't help but wonder how many of his girlfriends had pulled their hair out over this man-child thing he had going on. Probably plenty.

Crossing her arms over her chest, she walked over to the living room hearth, which was full of baseball memorabilia. Autographed cards and baseballs in display cases, and an old Yankees jersey hanging above the fireplace in a shadow box. It was impressive. She'd always loved baseball, but she was also fascinated by the history of it. Owen's hearth was like a miniature museum, and she reached up to touch the corner of one of the framed cards.

"Nolan Ryan," he said behind her. "My first love."

She turned to see him standing there, hands in his pockets. He wore a white button-down shirt tonight, the collar open at the throat. The sleeves were rolled up to reveal his tanned, muscled forearms.

"The coffee's brewing," he said. "Are you cold? You look cold."

She wasn't cold, but she was definitely shivering. She was so turned on and so anxious about it that she had to work to keep her teeth from chattering.

"I'm okay."

"Here." He grabbed a sweater from the arm of the couch and draped it over her shoulders. "Just in case."

Its softness felt good on her bare skin, and she could smell his scent in its fibers. She pulled it close. "Thank you. What a gentleman."

"Not really. What I'd like to do is take your clothes *off*, not add more to the mix."

Heat flooded her cheeks.

"God, I'm sorry." He shook his head. "Usually, I have more tact than that."

She could hardly believe that a man like Owen had just said that to her. But what she really couldn't believe was that Owen himself had just said it. Because out of any man in the world, he was the one she'd actually *let* take her clothes off.

"Why are you sorry?" she said, a small tremble in her voice. "I feel the same way."

At that, he gazed down at her, his jaw working. A heavy silence settled between them, and she could hear the coffee percolating from the kitchen. *Drip, drip, drip...* Its rich aroma filled her senses, reminding her of waking up in the mornings and lazing in bed. And at the thought of bed, her stomach curled.

"Wow," he finally said. Then he swallowed visibly, his Adam's apple bobbing up and down. "Okay. I wasn't expecting that."

She watched him. As hard as her heart was pounding, she knew if anything was going to happen between them tonight, he was going to have to make the first move. She'd thrown him a line; now he'd have to bite. And maybe between the two of them, he'd turn out to be the reasonable one. The one who would actually consider the potential fallout, because she wasn't considering much right then except the curve of his mouth.

"I have to be honest with you, Marley…"

He didn't step forward, just stayed right where he was, with his hands still firmly in his pockets. Definitely not where she'd fantasized them to be by now.

Her heart sank. Okay, maybe he really was going to be the reasonable one here. And that was a good thing. A single lust-filled night might look good in the pages of *Cosmo*, but in real life, they rarely ended well. Or she *assumed* they rarely ended well. She'd never actually had a one-night stand before. She'd always been too sensible for that.

He cleared his throat, and when he spoke again, his voice was husky. "I'm not looking for any kind of relationship right now," he said. "This is my last shot at the majors, and I can't afford to mess it up like I did in college."

If there was one thing she understood, it was not wanting to mess things up. She'd worked too hard for that, too. But she reminded herself that they were both adults here. Couldn't they just decide to have this one night together, quench this crazy thirst and then move on? As far as relationships went, they were in the same boat. She didn't want one, either. Or have time for one, for that matter. She might just be his perfect match. At least for the next few hours.

She raised her chin, starting to feel some of her confidence easing its way back. He wanted her, and she wanted him. And if the only thing standing in their way was setting a few ground rules, then she could live with that.

"I feel exactly the same," she said.

"You do?"

She nodded. "The last thing I want is to get involved with someone right now. I'm too focused on my career."

"Amen to that."

"But that doesn't mean…"

He raised his eyebrows. "That doesn't mean what?"

"Well. You know."

Seducing him was turning out to be harder than she thought. She wanted to be sexy and bold, but she just didn't have a ton of experience in that department.

She took a deep breath and started again. "We both feel the same way about not wanting to get involved. But we're both attracted to each other…"

"Saying I'm attracted to you would be an understatement at this point, but go on."

She smiled. "We're both attracted to each other, so what's wrong with a…a, uh…"

"A one-night stand?"

"Right. That."

She could see the pulse pounding in his neck from where she stood. Her gaze was drawn there like the spot was magnetized. Suddenly, all she could think about was placing her lips there, breathing in his scent, basking in his warmth.

"Let me get this straight," he said evenly. "You want to sleep with me?"

She felt a distinctive heat move up her neck and into her cheeks. "Basically. Yes."

"But you don't want any strings attached."

"I think that's important."

He nodded slowly.

"But I also think if we did this, if we…"

"Slept together?"

He was teasing her now. His blue eyes sparkled underneath the soft living room lights. Maybe he was just enjoying seeing her blush. God knew she was doing enough of it to last a lifetime.

"Yes. But if we did, I think it should only be this one time, don't you?"

He rubbed the back of his neck. "I'm not sure. I've never negotiated sex before."

She laughed. "Am I taking all the fun out of it?"

"Never. You're just being smart. Honestly, you're too good for me, Marley."

She'd always thought it was the other way around. But the way he was looking at her now almost made her believe he meant it.

"I'm not too good for you," she said. "And I don't know that I'm so much smart as realistic. I mean, we're adults. There's no reason it has to be complicated."

He rubbed the golden scruff on his chin. "Right, right. But what if I end up falling in love with you?"

At that, she stared up at him. And then she recognized that twinkle in his eyes, the teasing look she was getting to know so well. And she had to remind herself that love wasn't going to be a part of this equation. He clearly knew it, and she did, too. And if she was tempted to see him as anything other than a friend with benefits, well then. She'd have to remind herself again.

"I don't think you have to worry," she said. "I'm not *that* irresistible."

His expression grew serious again, and he took a step forward. "I'm not so sure about that."

Reaching out, he slid the sweater off her shoulders. His fingers brushed her bare skin, leaving goose bumps in their wake. His hands were impossibly sexy—long, blocky fingers, thick bone and tanned skin. They looked strong, capable. Just like the rest of him.

"I don't think we need this anymore," he said. "Do you? I've got other ways of keeping you warm."

And just like that, the last of her nerves melted away as those hands rested gently on her hips. And the question of whether or not this was a good idea was forgotten. Whatever the consequences, whatever the fallout, she could handle it.

At least, that was the last thought that ran through her mind as he bent close and placed his lips on hers.

## Chapter Four

Owen picked up the Louisville Slugger and tapped it once on each toe of his cleats, his most important ritual. He hadn't done it before that game with USC, and he'd lost his scholarship a week later. He'd forgotten to do it the first game of his sophomore year in high school, and his mother died a month later. Superstitious? Yeah. But it was what it was.

He held the bat tight and swung it through the misty air a few times, feeling the muscles in his shoulders loosen up with the familiar movement. Just being on the field had a way of relaxing his entire body, but it had taken longer than usual to get to that point today.

A few feet away, Max tossed a ball into the air and caught it in his glove with a soft smack. The rest of the team was just now trickling onto the field. Nobody was super stoked about practicing in this weather, but that was what you got when you played for a team on the Oregon Coast. Weather was just going to be part of the equation.

"So, are you going to tell me what happened last night?" Max said, his mop of curly hair sticking out from underneath the blue Tiger Sharks cap. "Or am I gonna have to hear it from someone else?"

Owen sliced the bat through the air again. "Don't know what you're talking about, man."

"*Liar.* I know you too well."

"Apparently you don't know me as well as you think, if you're assuming I'll tell you anything about last night." The tips of Owen's ears burned. Usually, ribbing like this didn't faze him, but today was different.

It wasn't that he didn't want to announce to the world that he'd slept with Marley. Who wouldn't? She was incredible in every way. But he doubted his coach would look favorably on this. And the *last* thing he needed was his teammates knowing about it. Besides, he was in the process of putting the whole thing behind him, anyway. That was what Marley wanted. And that was what he'd said he wanted, too. They'd been pretty clear about it.

The problem was, he couldn't get her out of his mind.

"You're so full of it," Max said, tossing the ball and catching it again. "But I'm not going to push, because I'm not sure you'd be able to take the stress in your geriatric state."

Teasing about his age. This, he was used to.

He smiled over at his friend. "Get bent, Maximus."

"I'm just saying. We need to take it easy on you. Respect our elders and all that."

Coach stepped out of the dugout, pulling his cap low over his eyes. He wore a blue windbreaker, had a clipboard tucked underneath one arm and was chewing a wad of gum, his only vice.

"Okay, folks," he said, clapping his hands. "Huddle up! We have a few announcements, and then we'll get this show on the road. It's supposed to dump later, and I'd rather be home when it does."

Owen set the bat down and headed over with the rest of the team. The wind had picked up since stepping onto the field half an hour ago, and he could hear the waves pounding the beach a few blocks away. It was one of those spring storms that would probably get worse before it got better.

Coach stood on the mound surrounded by his assistants, one of whom was a woman named Grace. Like Marley, she was new, but unlike Marley, she had the job of telling the guys what to do. Owen liked her. She didn't take any of his crap.

"Okay," his coach said. "A couple things. First off, thanks to everyone who came out last night. Sorry I burned that second batch of burgers. I put too much starter in."

The entire team gave a collective *boo*.

Coach smiled and pulled his hat lower over his eyes. "All right, all right. Barbecue isn't my strong suit."

There was another gust of wind, and the giant Coke sign next to first base flapped dramatically.

"Okay," Coach said, "I'll get on with it before we have to swim out of here. We've heard through the grapevine that some scouts will be here once the games get underway. We have some exceptional talent on this team, so this isn't a surprise."

Max gave Owen a knowing look. He was convinced Owen was going to get picked up this season, but Owen tried not to think too much about it. The only thing he could do was put in the work and hope for the best. And keep tapping the hell out of his cleats, of course.

But scouts were always a good thing. They were in the business of making dreams come true. Of bringing players to that magical and coveted place called "the show." These opportunities were what the minors were all about, and Owen himself had been waiting a very long time for this.

Standing there in the mist and wind, he felt his heart beat heavily inside his chest. He thought of Marley last night, her body so soft and giving underneath his. He thought of how she'd looked up at him with such warmth in her eyes, even after he'd told her he didn't want anything more. He couldn't help but wonder where her head was today. He didn't want to be a regret for her. He wanted to be the friend he'd meant to be in the first place, that he should've been in high school. They barely knew each other, but he cared about her. He cared what she thought of him.

Clenching his jaw, he looked over at the announcer's box, wondering how it was that he'd gotten here.

Six weeks into the season, and it had been another good game. Another really good game, and when Owen had stepped off the mound tonight to the roar of the crowd after pitching so many shutouts he was starting to lose track, it felt like he might actually have a shot at something bigger.

He walked out of the locker room with an aching arm but a swollen ego as a group of people stood waiting for his autograph.

Smiling, he began signing shirts and cards, and taking selfies with a few women in Tiger Sharks jerseys and not much else. His teammates pushed past, congratulating him on the game. The smell of hot dogs and warm pretzels filled his senses, and the cement was sticky underneath his shoes. He took it in, all of it. Wondering how it might feel, how things might look and smell in Yankee Stadium or Wrigley Field. Making it to the big leagues had been a dream of his for so long, sometimes it felt like that was all there was.

But of course, that was not all there was. And that

small realization was getting harder and harder to ignore. A splinter working its way underneath his skin. He was older than his teammates now, and eventually, he'd be too old. And then what? Would he enter the next phase of his life never having grown close to anyone or having nurtured any kind of meaningful relationships? It was a thought that kept coming back to him since being picked up by the Tiger Sharks. And since that night with Marley, it had settled into his very bones.

Handing a signed baseball card back to a grinning tween boy, he adjusted his duffel bag over his shoulder.

Max walked by and slapped him on the back. "Nice work, gramps. A bunch of us are going to the Pump House. Want to come? Celebrate that arthritic arm?"

Owen smiled, a smart-ass reply on the tip of his tongue, when he saw Marley making her way down the stairs from the announcer's box. She was wearing slacks and a cream-colored blouse, nothing mind-boggling, but his blood warmed just the same.

"I'll catch up with you," he said, watching her.

Max followed his gaze. "Oh, I get it."

"Nothing to get."

"No offense, but she doesn't seem that into you, bro."

Max had no idea how into him she'd been a few weeks ago. So into him that she'd left nail marks on his back. But that was then, and this was now. They were friends. That was it. And as her friend, he wanted to go say hi and ask how her day had been.

"She's not," he said. "And that's cool."

"Since when?"

"Since… I don't know. Since women aren't the only thing on my mind right now."

Max snorted. "Okay."

He had to admit, that sounded ridiculous to him, too. But Max was already headed toward the gates with a few of the other guys. "We'll save you a seat!" he said with a wave.

Owen watched them go, mingling with the last of the fans, who were headed toward their cars in the parking lot.

He looked back toward the announcer's box, half expecting to see Marley gone by now, but she was standing at the base of the stairs, digging for something in her purse.

Holding on to the strap of his duffel bag, he headed toward her with his heart beating heavily inside his chest. What he'd told Max just now was true. He did have things on his mind other than women. He hadn't said anything about one woman in particular, though, who had been on his mind plenty.

She looked up when she saw him and smiled. She was so beautiful that, for a second, he forgot the whole friends thing and was tempted to take her in his arms right then and there.

"Look who it is," she said, her voice a little raspy. "The star of the show."

He bowed dramatically.

"Seriously impressive, Owen," she continued. "Congratulations."

Straightening, he eyed her for a minute. "Are you getting sick? You sound congested."

"I do? Maybe it's because of calling the game. I always get kind of hoarse afterward."

"What were you looking for?" he asked.

"Looking for?"

He pointed to her purse.

"Oh." She cleared her throat. "Just a Tums. I made the mistake of having the nachos pregame."

"Oh yeah?"

"My stomach hates me now."

He smiled. "Can I walk you to your car? Like the gentleman that you think I am?"

"I'd love that. But I heard some of the guys are going to the Pump House. Aren't you going?"

"I'll meet them there. I wanted to catch up with you first."

"See? Total gentleman."

"If you say so."

She put her purse over her shoulder but then closed her eyes, swaying a little.

"Whoa, whoa, whoa." He stepped forward and grabbed her elbow. "You okay?"

She nodded, touching her temple. "I'm fine. Just got a little dizzy there for a second."

"Here, why don't you sit down? You look pale."

She sat without arguing, and he sat next to her.

"I'm okay," she said. "Really. You don't have to stay."

"A gentleman wouldn't leave you sitting here by yourself, looking like you're gonna pass out."

She appeared startled. "Do I really look like that?"

"A little."

She rubbed her temple again. "Great."

"So, what's going on?"

"I think I'm just tired. Maybe a little stressed."

"A little?"

"Okay. A lot." She gave him a small smile. "I love my job, but there's some pressure to perform. I haven't been sleeping great."

He could understand that. More than she probably knew. Despite how well these last few games had gone, he'd been sleeping like crap, too. When people expected you to crash and burn, there was a significant amount of fear that you actually would.

"And I've been worrying about Frances," she continued. "Things are working right now, but what about six months from now? What about a year from now?" She chewed the inside of her cheek. "I don't know. I guess I'm just having trouble turning it all off."

Her hand was resting on her thigh, a few inches from his. She was leaning into him, just the smallest bit, and he could feel the warmth from her body. He thought about how she'd felt a few weeks ago, after he'd unzipped that dress. So soft, so warm, and she'd smelled so good. He'd leaned down and moved her hair away from her neck to kiss it. He could almost taste her now.

He swallowed hard. He could definitely understand not being able to turn it off.

She turned to him, her face, her lips, only inches from his. "I'm just so proud of you," she said. "What a game."

So, they were going to talk about baseball. Okay. He could do that. He could keep from leaning in and kissing her, because she'd probably push him away and remind him of their agreement, and she'd be absolutely right.

"Thanks," he said. "I'm trying not to think about all that's riding on this. Just trying to enjoy the experience."

"Well, I know about the scouts," she said. "You're getting noticed."

That was what he'd heard, too. But it was too early in the season to obsess about it. He was too superstitious for that, anyway. He'd been down that road before.

Looking down at his hands, he clasped them together, his elbows resting on his knees. "I just want something more, you know?"

He felt her watching him. For some reason, he said things to Marley that he'd never think about saying to anyone else. She made him feel calm, peaceful. He'd never had that with a woman before. Not really.

"You were always meant for more," she said.

He looked over at her.

"You have a gift, Owen."

He thought some of the color might be coming back into her cheeks. She was lovely underneath the lights of the ballpark, with soft shadows underneath her eyes and next to her cheekbones. His heart ached. What a beauty.

He looked back down at his hands, squeezing them together. "Sometimes I wonder where I'd be if I hadn't screwed up in college. Probably not back in Christmas Bay."

"Would you rather not be here?"

He shrugged. "I don't know that I would've come back if the Sharks hadn't picked me up. But now that I'm here…it's not like I thought it would be."

"And how's that?"

"Not terrible."

She laughed. "Well, that's good."

"You know what I mean, though. Would you have ever come back if it weren't for your foster mother?"

She seemed to consider this, looking out toward the bleachers. "No. I don't think I would've."

"And now?"

"Now?" She lowered her lashes. "It's not terrible."

They sat there for a minute listening as the maintenance crew began their cleanup of the park. Hearing the waves crash in the distance. It was nice sitting here next to her. Even though he was still tempted to kiss her, he was enjoying just being close to her. And that was new for him.

Finally, she looked over again, watching him closely. "Did you always know you wanted to be a baseball player? When you were little?"

He thought about that. Reaching back into the furthest crevices of his mind, where his faintest memories were. And he saw himself as a kid, wanting his parents' attention and doing anything he could think of to get it. Baseball had been the easiest way to get his father to notice him. But it hadn't lasted.

He pulled in a deep breath, letting it saturate his lungs before answering. A necessity when talking about his childhood.

"At first, it was just a way of fitting in," he said. "And then I found out I was actually good, and people started noticing me. My parents seemed to care what I did. At least for a while. And then I was hooked. I loved everything about it. The fit of the glove and the smell of the grass. The way it felt when I hit a homer. The way the crowd sounded...all of it. It gave me purpose. And I hadn't had a lot of purpose growing up."

She nodded.

"I don't remember ever wanting to be anything else," he continued. "The older I got, the more I wanted to make it to the majors. It was all I could think about. All I ever cared about."

"And now?"

He ran his hands down his thighs, thinking about

that. Who was he if he wasn't a ball player? It was an unsettling thought, one that made him feel unanchored.

"It's my dream," he said simply.

She smiled. She looked so pretty right then that he wondered just how long he'd be able to abide by the rules they'd laid out. How long would it be before he gave in to this incredible urge to touch her again?

"What about you?" he asked, his voice husky. "Is there anything else you want besides your career?"

She seemed to think about that, gazing out over the park. "Just to be happy. It seems like I've been chasing baseball for so long, sometimes I wonder what it would be like to slow down a little."

"Learn to knit?"

She laughed. "Not exactly. But maybe explore life beyond baseball."

"*Is* there life beyond baseball?"

"For us? I guess not."

She seemed to be feeling better now. Definitely didn't look like she was going to pass out anymore.

"Hey," he said. "Speaking of slowing down... Do you fish?"

"I've never been. Why?"

"I bought my buddy's boat last fall, and now that the weather is getting warmer, I've been meaning to take it out on an inaugural trip. We've got tomorrow off. Want to come with me?"

"I don't..."

"You said yourself you've been stressed. Getting out on a boat is a great way to relax, I'm telling you."

She smiled slowly.

"I promise, it'll be strictly platonic," he said. "Fishing only. That's it."

"I do love being on the water."

"Then it's a date?"

"It's a date."

Marley walked through the door of her town house and tossed her keys on the table. Her head still felt swimmy, off. But it was the churning of her stomach that made her go directly to the couch and sit down with a sigh. She wished she could go back and chuck those stupid nachos right in the garbage can.

Leaning her head back on the cushion, she kicked her shoes off. She was tired. More than that, she was exhausted. What she'd told Owen tonight was true—she *was* worried about Frances, and stressed about work. She'd always been a type A personality, and that was never more apparent than when the season got into full swing. Everything had to be perfect—her voice, her delivery, all of it. But she kept reminding herself that nobody was perfect, not even the announcers in the majors, and she'd just have to settle for doing the best she could. After all, it seemed to be working so far.

Still, tonight, she felt like death warmed up, and

she wished that, along with throwing the nachos away, she'd told Owen that she didn't feel up to fishing in the morning. But he'd been practically irresistible with that teasing twinkle in his eyes, with that gorgeous smile, meant just for her. How could she possibly say no?

Honestly, she hadn't wanted to. She simply wanted to be in his vicinity, to soak him in like a drug that she couldn't seem to get enough of. She'd slowly found that one-night-stands weren't nearly as simple as she'd hoped they would be. At least, this one wasn't.

She pulled her feet up and covered herself with a buttery soft throw that she kept draped on the back of the couch for nights like this, when she couldn't seem to drag herself into the bedroom. The throw felt especially good at the moment. Even though the late-May evening was warmer than usual, she'd felt achy and cold since leaving Owen and climbing into her car. Leaving him lately was enough to make her feel cold, but maybe she was coming down with something. Great. She remembered Frances telling her a bug was going around the community center last week. She made a mental note to take some Airborne before Owen picked her up in the morning.

Closing her eyes, she rolled over and hugged one of the throw pillows to her stomach, hoping the nausea would pass soon. She hated feeling like this. If she didn't know better, she'd think she was—

Her eyes shot open. She stared out the darkened window, but didn't see the stars twinkling overhead. In fact, she wasn't aware of anything but the sound of the blood rushing in her ears. *If I didn't know better, I'd think I was...what?*

She sat up slowly, unable to finish that thought. Because finishing that thought would only lead to panic. To pulling out the calendar in the kitchen and calculating how many days it had been exactly since she and Owen had slept together. To stumbling out to her car and driving half an hour to the next town over, trying to find a drugstore that was open, because she knew the two here were closed and wouldn't open up until ten the next morning.

She blinked, vaguely aware that she'd thrown the blanket off. She wasn't cold anymore. She was very, very hot, which had everything to do with the fact that she was panicking anyway, despite her best efforts otherwise.

She hiccuped and touched her fingers to her lips. Then she got up and ran to the bathroom, not thinking of anything else except making it there in time to throw up.

## Chapter Five

Marley sat in the passenger seat of Owen's truck, gripping the door handle as they bounced over another rut in the dirt road.

"Sorry about that," he said. "We're almost there. It's bumpier than I remembered."

She forced a smile, but was desperate for some fresh air.

Cracking the window, she leaned toward the early-morning breeze that instantly cooled her forehead and cheeks. *That's better*, she told herself. *Just breathe...*

But breathing was turning out to be harder than she thought. Since last night. Since falling into a troubled, bone-weary sleep, after realizing that her period was most definitely late.

"You okay?" Owen glanced over, his blond eyebrows knitted together.

He looked so sexy this morning in his heathergray hoodie and UCLA baseball cap that it was easy to be distracted by him. And that was exactly why she'd ended up coming this morning. She needed distraction. Badly. At least until she could get her hands on a pregnancy test.

"I'm okay," she managed. "Just a little carsick."

"Uh-oh. You're never going to agree to come fishing with me again."

She actually had no idea how she was going to handle being in a boat. The truck ride alone was enough of a challenge.

Looking out the window, she took another deep breath. It was a gorgeous morning. Chilly in the shade, but bright and clear, with only a few puffy white clouds at the base of the mountains. Giant evergreens stood sentry on either side of the road, and the small lake in the distance was a sparkling sapphire blue that mirrored the sky overhead. She just wished she could enjoy it more.

She readjusted the seat belt against her neck, trying to concentrate on the chafing there instead of the tight, slightly achy feeling in her lower belly. That might just be her imagination. But ever since the word *pregnant* had popped into her head, she'd been having a hard time imagining anything else. They'd used a condom. Actually, they'd used several condoms that night. She wasn't on any kind of birth control because she hadn't dated anyone since AJ. But sitting here now, she wished she had the extra peace of mind that birth control pills would've given her. Condoms didn't break very often, but they did break, and the end result was...

She shifted in her seat. Again.

"I love it out here," Owen said, maneuvering the truck around another rut in the road. "My dad took me fishing here a few times, and it was the only place he ever seemed happy. He sure as hell wasn't happy at home."

"I think I remember your parents were divorced?"

"They broke up when I was little. My mom died when I was in high school."

She swallowed hard, her mouth suddenly dry. Something else they had in common. No mothers. "I'm so sorry."

He kept his eyes on the road, his baseball cap pulled low over his eyes. "She had problems, but she was my mom. And at least with her, I had a family. When she died, I went to live with my dad, and that was pretty much hell."

She thought of her own father then. She remembered trying so hard to make him happy. Thinking if she cooked dinner the way he liked it or cleaned the house the right way or got straight A's, he'd finally be proud of her. Kinder to her. See something in her worth loving. But nothing ever worked. He'd always come home just as mean and resentful as when he'd left. And eventually he hadn't come home at all.

The muscles in Owen's jaw bunched and then relaxed as he watched the dirt road ahead. "Ancient history," he said. "But at least he gave me my love of fishing."

Marley pulled the sleeves of her sweatshirt over her hands, an old childhood habit. "My dad gave me nothing at all."

She hadn't meant to go there. And now that the words were hanging between them, the mood in the truck felt heavier. She wished she could suck them back in.

Frowning, he looked over at her. "Parents can really screw you over, can't they?"

"At least I had Frances," she said. "It took me a long time to trust anyone after my dad, but I got there eventually. If I hadn't had my foster family, I'm not sure what would've happened to me."

"I'm sorry," he said. And his voice, the tone of it, was like a salve being put on a burn. It soothed her, eased the pain, just a little.

"I don't normally talk about it, but for some reason, you make it easy."

"I don't know that I believe that," he said. "I know it's hard for you. It's hard for me, too. But maybe it's easier with each other than it would be with anyone else."

"Yes. That."

He smiled. "The good thing is that it's behind us,

right? We didn't have a choice back then, but we do now. I'm never having kids."

Her stomach, which had already been queasy, dropped like a lead weight. She licked her lips and sat up straighter in her seat, hoping the feeling would pass in a minute.

"Oh?" she said, forcing herself to sound casual. *Kids? What kids?*

"No way. Knowing how much you can mess up? No way in hell."

She stared straight ahead. Just because her period was late did not mean she was pregnant. She'd been late plenty of times. Plus, she was stressed with her new job, the move and trying to help Frances. All those things could affect her cycle. She knew that.

Still, as she sat beside him, doing her best to stay calm, she also knew she'd never been this late before. And she'd never felt quite like this, either. Nauseated, but it was a different kind of nausea. There was a metallic taste in her mouth, a tightness in her belly and lower back. She just felt...*off*.

He looked over at her again. "What's wrong?"

"Nothing."

"Does it bother you that I said I don't want kids?"

"Why would it bother me?"

"I don't know," he said. "I don't want you to think I'm an asshole."

"I wouldn't think that."

The truth was, she didn't know what to think. She

couldn't seem to contemplate his words, let alone the possibility of a broken condom. The more she thought about it, the woozier she got.

"How close are we?" she asked, leaning toward the cracked window again.

"About ten minutes. Why?"

"Can you pull over for a second? I think I need to get out, get some fresh air."

"Sure."

He pulled the truck over at a wide spot in the road and cut the engine. The dust settled around them, and they were immediately enveloped in the stillness of the forest.

Marley opened the door and stepped out. Burying her hands in her sweatshirt pocket, she pulled the cool air into her lungs. This was better, she thought, as her heartbeat began to slow. This was much better.

Owen got out, too, and walked around his truck to where she stood. The edge of the lake was only a few yards away, and a woodpecker tapped busily above their heads. It smelled good out here, fresh. Like pine trees and wildflowers. It had been a long time since she'd spent any time in the woods. When she, Stella and Kyla were teenagers, Frances used to take them on picnics, but it had been a few years since she'd indulged in one of those. Since she'd had time to indulge in one.

She made her way down the slight embankment to the gently lapping water. The sun was dappled and warm on her shoulders, filtering in through the canopy of trees like a long-lost friend.

She stood there, hearing Owen walk up behind her, and stared out over the lake.

He put a hand on her back, and its weight felt so good, so comforting, that she thought she might cry for a second.

"What's going on, Marley?" he asked, his voice low. "What's wrong?"

"Nothing. I'm okay."

"That's not true."

She racked her brain for something he might believe for now. Just to give herself some time to absorb this. She'd already told him she wasn't feeling great, that she was stressed out with work and life…

That was all true. She was dealing with a lot. And to make matters worse, AJ had called last night, telling her that he was coming out to the West Coast for a few days and wanted to swing by for a visit.

Normally, she'd be happy to see him—they'd been together a long time, and she still considered him a close friend. But when he'd hinted he wanted to give their relationship another shot, her heart sank. She didn't love AJ. In fact, she didn't think she ever had, not like he deserved to be loved. But that was definitely something she was going to have to tell him in person, and now, on top of everything else, she was dreading it.

She licked her lips, tasting the ChapStick there.

She'd just tell Owen she was anxious about seeing AJ. She *was* anxious. And that would pacify him for a while, until she could figure out what was going on with her body.

"It's just that I haven't felt great these last few days," she said, "and my ex-boyfriend is flying out for a visit, and we still have some things to work through."

He watched her. "What kinds of things?"

"I think he might want to get back together."

Slowly, he crossed his arms over his chest.

She looked over at him. Surely, that hadn't made him jealous? Owen was one of the most confident people she'd ever met, especially when it came to women. And she wasn't fooling herself that she stood out from the crowd in that department. She'd seen some of the girls gathered around the locker room after the games. They looked like supermodels, their bodies so toned and tight, even she had a hard time looking away.

But there was no denying the fact that he wasn't making eye contact now. And those muscles in his jaw were bunching again.

"Oh yeah?" he said. "How do you feel about that?"

"I love AJ. But I don't *love* AJ. We were never right for each other. He wants different things, and that's okay. But they're not what I want. We just don't work as a couple."

"Poor bastard."

She smiled, starting to feel a little better. Her stomach was beginning to settle. At least enough to consider getting in the boat, which was hitched expectantly to the truck behind them. It was a great boat. She really didn't want to get sick in it.

"I think he knows that deep down," she said. "He's just having a hard time accepting it. We were together so long that I'm a habit that's hard to break."

"I can understand that. I'd have a hard time walking away from you, too."

Her chest warmed. There was a part of her that would love to believe that. Imagine it, even. But that wasn't smart. She'd already let herself feel more for Owen than she was comfortable with.

"Speaking of too different," she said, nudging him in the elbow.

"Us? We're different, but that doesn't mean we don't mesh. We sure did that night."

She laughed. "Yes, but sex does not a relationship make. Or, at least, that's what Frances used to say to us in high school."

"It's a good jumping-off point, though. Hypothetically."

"It's backward."

"It's fun."

It was fun. She couldn't argue with that.

"So," he said slowly. "AJ, huh? Am I going to have to watch out for this guy? Make sure he's treating you right if you get back together?"

"We aren't getting back together."

"Now you sound like a Taylor Swift song."

She looked over at him. "You listen to Taylor Swift?"

"Of course. She's badass."

"Huh. I just figured you for more of a Led Zeppelin guy."

"I have eclectic tastes."

"Obviously."

"So, you're never, ever getting back together with AJ," he said.

"Nope."

"And I can't convince you to run away with me."

She smiled. "Not likely."

"So, you're just going to concentrate on your career and family, and break hearts in the process, right?"

"Basically."

He was teasing her, of course. But he couldn't have any idea that her heart was the one in danger of being broken. If he kept being so charming, if he kept being so handsome and sweet, her heart might do more than break. It might shatter into a hundred little pieces.

No, what she needed to do was keep her head on straight. She needed to stay calm until she could get herself to a drugstore. And in the meantime, she needed to keep her stupid heart in check. No matter what.

"So," he said, tugging on the rim of his baseball cap, "are you ready to catch some fish?"

She nodded. They'd catch some fish. And if she were lucky, she wouldn't toss her cookies.

"Are you going to tell me why you called me all the way over here, or am I going to have to tickle it out of you?"

Kyla was sitting on the edge of the coffee table, her elbows on her knees, looking Marley directly in the eyes. Just like she had as a teenager, when she'd demanded to know everything going on in her foster sister's life. Only now, there was a sliver of worry there. And Marley knew why. She felt woozy, and probably looked a heck of a lot worse. Woozy with a side of ghostly pale, maybe?

Actually, she was surprised she was still able to sit upright at all since peeing on the little stick that was at that very moment seasoning on her bathroom counter.

Knowing she definitely couldn't wait for the results on her own, she'd called Kyla and asked her to come over. Quickly. Which Kyla had. Complete with a hastily-thrown-on outfit and no bra. She'd apparently been about to shower when the phone rang.

Marley took a deep breath, bringing her feet up underneath her. It was a gray evening with a strong wind that kept rattling the windows of the town house. Outside, the bay was choppy and dark, and the seagulls were having a hard time not being blown all over the sky. One of them stood on her balcony railing now,

his feathers ruffled around his neck and his little orange legs stiff as he tried to keep his balance.

*"Well?"* Kyla said.

"I don't know how to tell you this," Marley said.
"When I called you, I didn't really think it through.
How to tell you, that is. It was easier in my head."

Kyla waited, watching her with wide eyes. *Good
grief.* She just needed to spit it out. But it really had
been easier in her head.

"I think…" she began. Then licked her lips, and
said a little prayer for courage. But in her heart, she
knew it would be fine. A shock, for sure, but fine.
There was a reason she'd called Kyla instead of Stella
or Frances (bless them). She'd known Kyla would
keep her the calmest. And she wouldn't judge. Not
that Stella would judge, but Stella would immediately be defensive of Marley, and would most likely
skewer Owen, because she was the big sister.

As for Frances? Well, Marley guessed her foster
mother probably hadn't had a meaningless fling to
compare this to. She'd been married to a wonderful
man, the absolute love of her life, until he'd passed
away right before Marley had come to live with her.
Since then, she'd been so busy with the house and
the candy shop that she hadn't had time for romance.
Not that anyone would ever come close to Bud, anyway. He was her one and only. Marley knew Frances
wouldn't judge, either, but it might be harder for her
to wrap her mind around this.

So, she'd called Kyla. The one who stayed calm in a crisis. Marley swallowed hard. Was this a crisis? She looked at the clock on the wall. She'd know in a few more minutes.

"You think what?" Kyla asked, trying to get her to finish her sentence already.

*Here goes...*

"I think I might be pregnant," she said evenly.

Kyla's mouth hung open. For several awful seconds, the silence between them was deafening. But it wasn't actually deafening, because Marley thought she could hear the beating of her own heart.

*"What?"* Kyla asked. "What did you just say?"

"I think I might be—"

"Never mind. I heard that part. How? How are you pregnant? Don't answer that, either. I mean, I know *how.* Did you go see AJ? I had a feeling he wasn't going to give up that easy. But you don't love him, Marls. You said so yourself. That's what you said, right? I mean, I'm not imagining that part?"

Poor Kyla. It looked like her head was about to explode. Although, Marley had to hand it to her. She wasn't freaking out. Yet. She was just really, really...confused.

"It's not AJ's," she said. "If there *is* a baby, which I'm not sure there is yet. I'm waiting on the test." She gestured toward the bathroom.

Kyla's gaze flickered over her shoulder, and then

back again. She closed her eyes briefly and touched her hand to her temple. "I feel like I'm dreaming this."

"Tell me about it."

"If it's not AJ...then who?"

Marley clasped her hands in her lap. "Owen Taylor."

Her foster sister jumped to her feet and gaped down at her. *"What?"*

"I know. I'm sorry I didn't tell you. I'm so sorry, Kyla, but I didn't tell anyone. And I especially couldn't say anything to you and Frances and Stella after that whole night at Mario's."

"Yes, I remember," Kyla said. "The night when you said you couldn't stand him."

"I couldn't stand him. That was the truth."

"But you slept with him! What in the world happened between that night and..." She did a quick calculation with her fingers, presumably counting the weeks off. "It's almost June. If you're just now thinking you might be pregnant, you slept together when?"

"Remember that work party I told you about?"

"The party you bought the black dress for."

"That's the one."

Kyla slowly sat back down. The shocked expression was beginning to wear off. "Well, I knew you looked fantastic in that dress. I knew it. It's no wonder he couldn't resist you."

Marley laughed, and it felt like some of the tension was finally beginning to ease from her shoulders. *This*. She'd needed this. To laugh with one of her sisters, to confide in her. To share this deeply personal, profoundly terrifying turn of events in her life.

"It might've been the other way around," she said. "There was a lot of passion. I'll just put it that way."

Kyla grinned. "So, we've established that the sex was good. But how about the man? How do you feel about this guy?"

That was the million-dollar question. How did she feel about Owen? It was only supposed to be that one night, and they'd agreed to be friends afterward. Like two reasonable adults who'd grown to care about each other. But the truth was more complicated than that, as the truth usually was. She felt like she could fall for Owen. More than that, she felt like she already was falling for him, and that, like having to take this pregnancy test tonight, hadn't exactly been part of her plan.

She rubbed her lips together, wondering if she could even say these things out loud yet. They were scary enough to think about, let alone utter to someone else. Even to Kyla, who was looking at her so tenderly. With such excitement and hope.

"He's changed so much," she said. "And I like him. I really like him, but he's got his career, and I've got mine, and we aren't looking for anything else."

"Except…"

"I know. Except possible *parenthood*."

"Oh, honey," Kyla said, reaching for her hand.

"I'm just glad you called. I know how you feel. Ben and I actually had a pregnancy scare a few months ago, and I was beside myself. A complete mess."

"You never told me that."

Kyla was dating Christmas Bay's police chief, and was even talking about moving in with him and his six-year-old daughter, whom she was crazy about. They were happy. Really happy. And their relationship gave Marley hope that happily-ever-afters really did exist.

"I didn't want to worry you. You were getting ready for the move and the new job. You had enough going on."

"Did you tell Ben?"

"I did, and he was wonderful, as usual. Actually, I think he might've been a little disappointed when we found out I wasn't pregnant."

Marley's heart squeezed. He was a good guy.

"Anyway," Kyla said, "I think it happened for a reason. It helped us realize what we really want."

"And what's that?"

"To be a family. When we're ready for it."

*A family.* Like those happily-ever-afters, she had to remind herself that complete families happened, too. Just because she and her foster sisters hadn't had a traditional one, that didn't mean they didn't exist. It didn't mean they wouldn't find one someday.

She felt the smile fade on her lips. But was that what she wanted? It was so much responsibility. And she didn't know if she had what it took to be a good mother, anyway.

Kyla looked up at the clock. "I'm sure that test is ready by now. Are you?"

Her stomach knotted. "No. But I'll go check anyway."

"I'll be right here."

She stood, her legs quivering underneath her. It was going to be okay. Whatever that little test said, it was going to be okay.

She kept telling herself that over and over again as she walked into the cheerful bathroom with the violet towels and flowered shower curtain that she'd picked out at TJ Maxx a few months ago.

Biting the inside of her cheek, she said another prayer and looked down at the strip on the counter.

There was a little plus sign in the window.

Owen settled onto the rowing machine in the clubhouse's small gym and gripped the handles with tight fists. He'd come in early to work out before the game, something he did when he needed to think. There was nobody here except his coach, who was in his office. He'd just called Owen in, and the news was good.

It looked like the scouts who had come the other night were interested. It was too early to be expecting any offers yet, but his coach was confident that several would be coming by midseason. He wanted

Owen to think about what he wanted, where he wanted to end up if he had more than one choice. It was surreal. But that wasn't what he was thinking about now, as a light sweat began to prickle his skin. It was Marley.

Leaning forward, he pushed the button to increase the tension and began working out in earnest. His shoulder and thigh muscles burned with the effort. He moved faster, harder, as he pictured Marley standing at the edge of the lake the other day, looking like she was about to cry. What he'd wanted to do was pull her into his arms and hold her close. Lean down and smell her hair, feel the warmth of her skin next to his. But like the coward he was, he'd kept his distance. Turned out that was a good thing, too, since the next words out of her mouth had been about her ex-boyfriend coming to see her.

Owen wiped the sweat off his forehead and scowled up at the TV, where some news show was playing on mute. He hadn't been prepared for how that information would affect him. Something that shouldn't have had any bearing on his mood at all had made him want to climb right out of his skin. And now here he was. About to break this stupid rowing machine.

He forced even breaths and eased up a little, not wanting to give himself a damn heart attack before the game even started. But he couldn't stop thinking about Marley and the fact that this guy wanted to give their relationship another shot. Whatever the hell that meant. But he knew what it meant. The guy was probably still in love with her, and who wouldn't be? And even though she said she didn't love him back, she might be tempted to get back together with him anyway.

It all felt like more than Owen could take. But take it he would. Because even though they'd slept together, and even though she'd occupied nearly all of his waking thoughts since, he was in no position to compete for her. He was just going to have to get over this ridiculous jealousy. He was too busy for it anyway.

That was what he kept telling himself as the sweat began to trickle between his shoulder blades, and the muscles in his legs quivered with fatigue.

"Gramps!"

He looked over to see Max walk in with his duffel bag slung over his shoulder.

"You're here early," his friend said. "What gives?"

"Just wanted to get a workout in before the game."

Max set his bag down beside the free weights, then sat with a sigh. His mop of curly hair was everywhere today. He looked like he'd just rolled out of bed.

"You know," he said, "I give you a hard time about being old and everything, but I'm feeling it today, man. My back is killing me."

Owen smiled. "You might have to ask for some therapy after the game."

"Yeah. I was thinking the same thing."

The team's physical therapist was a tall brunette named Denise. Max had a thing for her. A major thing. In fact, he followed her around like a puppy whenever the opportunity presented itself, which was often.

Max touched his ear to his shoulder, and his neck cracked. "Did you hear that? I'm falling apart."

"Nothing Denise can't fix."

"I don't know. I don't think she's into me, man. I'm trying so hard, but the harder I try, the more she retreats. Like, she practically runs away when she sees me coming."

Owen wiped the sweat from his forehead again. "There's your problem. You're trying too hard. Let her come to you."

"Easy for you to say," Max said. "I'm not as hot as you. I can't just sit back and wait until they flock to me."

"Nobody flocks to me."

"Right. Riiiight. They only wait for you outside the locker room in droves."

Okay. That might be true. But it was also true that for the last few weeks, he hadn't noticed it as much. And that definitely wasn't like him.

Max seemed to be thinking the same thing, because he narrowed his eyes at him. "There's something different about you, and I can't put my finger on it. Wait. That's bull. I *can* put my finger on it."

Owen rowed a little harder.

"I think there's something going on between you and Marley Carmichael," Max said, pointing at him. "You won't admit it, but ever since she showed up, you haven't been able to take your eyes off her. It's so obvious, man. Why don't you just tell me what's going on?"

Glancing up at the TV, Owen tried to look interested in what was on. At the moment, it was a tampon commercial. "Why are you so interested, anyway?"

"Because we're friends, and friends talk to each other about these things. We are friends, aren't we?"

"Yeah, we're friends."

"Then tell me what's up with you. Seriously."

Owen leaned forward and turned the rower off. Then leaned back in the seat and sighed. "Okay. You're right."

"I'm right? There's something going on between you two?"

"There's nothing going on between us. Not really. But I do like her."

Max smiled slowly. "That's great, man. Congrats."

"For what? We're not dating or anything."

"Why not?"

Owen swept his hand in a wide arc. "Because of this. Because of all of this. I'm too busy, and I don't want to get sidetracked by a relationship."

Max rolled his eyes. "Come on."

"What?"

"I know you're elderly and everything, but that's so dated. There are a lot of guys with wives and girlfriends, with families, who make it work."

"There are—you're right. But there are a lot who don't."

"Just because you had a bad experience, like a thousand years ago, doesn't mean you have to swear off relationships forever, Taylor."

Owen reached for his towel and draped it over his neck. "As you love to point out, I'm older than all of you. This isn't my first rodeo, remember? There's a reason I haven't settled down, and it's not because of one or two experiences. It's because it can change the entire trajectory of your career."

"Uh-huh," Max said, ignoring that completely. "So, what's wrong with her? She seems great to me. Or are you just intentionally turning your back on something good?"

Owen rubbed his jaw. "I don't see myself sacrificing baseball for anyone, that's all."

"Well, not that you'd ever have to choose. But, man, I would."

Owen stared at him.

"Yeah," Max said. "I'd sacrifice all this."

"Since when? You love baseball."

"Sure, I love it. But I don't have your arm, man. The minors are the last stop for me. If I met someone awesome...if they were the bread to my butter..."

Owen smiled.

"...then screw it," Max finished. "That's what's important at the end of the day. Finding someone to share your life with, right?"

Owen had had no idea his friend felt this way. And that was because he'd never thought to ask. It was a pattern that he wasn't proud of. Had he always been such an asshole?

"I hear you," he said slowly. "I do. But how would you feel if you got picked up by the majors tomorrow? Would you feel the same?"

"Yeah. Yeah, I think I would."

Owen considered this. Deep down, he knew Max was right. People mixed successful careers and relationships all the time. But even if he suddenly had a change of heart, Marley wasn't interested. They'd agreed on that. And now there was this ex-boyfriend in the mix who made things exponentially more complicated.

He stood up and grabbed his bag. A hot shower sounded good. He needed to get centered before the game, and this conversation wasn't helping. He'd been thinking about Marley before, having trouble getting her out of his head. But now it seemed like she'd lodged herself in his heart, too, and he wasn't quite sure what to do about that. It unsettled him.

"See you later, man," he said to Max as he passed. "Gotta shower."

"Hey."

Owen turned.

"I understand where you're coming from," Max said. "This is your dream. I get it. But there's room for more in life than just baseball."

Owen let that settle. It reminded him of what Marley had said the other day. And how he'd joked afterward, asking her if there were any such thing.

"You know," he said, "for such a baby, you might actually know what you're talking about."

"So, you're saying I'm smart?"

"I'm saying you're smarter than I thought you were."

"Not the *highest* praise…"

"See you on the field, Maximus."

"One more thing," Max said. "If you're not gonna ask Marley out, can I?"

Owen gave him a look.

"Whoa," Max said with a laugh. "Never mind."

## Chapter Six

Marley sat on the examining room table and adjusted the pink gown around her waist for what must have been the tenth time. She looked up at the clock. Her palms were sweaty and her stomach was weak, but that wasn't anything new lately.

She was pregnant. One hundred percent knocked up. Her doctor had just confirmed it, although not in those exact words, of course.

Now she was waiting for her first exam, when what she really wanted to do was go home and eat a gallon of Ben & Jerry's. The thought of anything else made her stomach turn, but for some reason, ice cream was just as tempting as always. A blessing. Her entire world was now standing on its head, but at least she still had ice cream.

The door opened and Dr. Binky walked in. He was an older balding man with kind brown eyes. He wore a bow tie and had been in obstetrics for over forty years. She was scared to death, had no clue what she was going to do next, but at least her doctor made her feel safe.

"How are we doing, Ms. Carmichael?" he said, patting her hand. "Is the news settling yet?"

She must've looked exactly how she felt, because he smiled and pulled up a chair.

"A little," she said. "I'm still having a hard time believing it."

"It's a lot to take in. I know you must have a lot of questions, and I want you to feel comfortable here with us. My team and I are going to be here for you every step of the way, all right?"

"Thank you."

"Christmas Bay General is top-notch," he continued. "So you can feel good about delivering there when the time comes. Or are you more interested in a home birth?"

Marley's tongue suddenly felt like a cotton ball inside her mouth. "I'm sorry," she said. "Can I have a drink of water, please?"

"Of course, of course." He stood up, filled a paper cup from the tap and handed it over. "Just take your time."

She took a couple of greedy swallows and then licked her lips. "Thank you."

He took the cup and tossed it in the trash can,

then turned to her with a frown. "I feel like I need to ask," he said. "Will you have support from friends or family? Pregnancy is taxing physically, but it can be even harder emotionally. We want to make sure your heart has what it needs, too, not just your body."

The words were like a warm hug. She had Frances, and she had Stella and Kyla. No matter what, they'd help get her through this. Even so, ever since she'd seen that plus sign in that little round window, she'd felt more alone than she ever had in her life. And she'd spent a lot of time feeling alone.

The backs of her eyes prickled with tears, and she hoped she wouldn't start crying in front of this nice man who looked so concerned for her.

She chewed the inside of her cheek and waited a few seconds to answer. "I have family," she said. "But the baby's father..."

He waited, watching her.

"The baby's father doesn't know yet. It's complicated, and I don't know how he's going to feel about this. To be honest, I'm terrified of telling him."

Dr. Binky patted her hand again. "I know this has to be incredibly difficult. But no matter what you decide to do, it will be the right choice for you."

She looked down at the pink smock, the tiny flower print reminding her of Frances's garden on the cape. When she was a girl, she used to be able to disappear inside that little garden, and all her troubles just seemed to melt away. She longed for that kind of innocence now. That kind of security. And tears filled her eyes.

"It's just overwhelming," she said, wiping them with the back of her hand. "I know it will work out, but there are so many things hanging in the balance…"

"There are. This is a lot of responsibility. But I can see how strong you are. Once you have a chance to get your mind around this, you'll figure it out. You will."

Marley let out a shaky breath. It was exactly what she needed to hear. She actually believed him when he said she'd figure it out. It wouldn't be easy, but she would.

She ran her hand down the gown and just hoped it would be sooner rather than later.

"A baby," Frances sighed dreamily. "I still can't believe I'm going to be a nana."

Marley let her hand fall to her belly and walked slowly along the beach next to her foster mother. It was a beautiful morning, with barely any wind at all. She'd discovered that the cool, salty air did wonders for her queasy stomach in the mornings, so she'd started meeting Frances for walks before work. It was nice.

"Don't get too excited, Frances," she said. "I'm not sure what I'm going to do yet."

"I know, honey. But whatever you decide, I'm still going to be a nana. There's still going to be a little

Marley out there somewhere, even if you do decide on adoption."

Marley's heart squeezed. Frances's support and love hadn't wavered for one second. If anything, it had only grown since Marley had broken the news. And her foster sisters had been just as wonderful, fussing over her daily, bringing her hot tea and take-out, until she thought she might pop if she ate one more bite of comfort food.

*You're eating for two now!* Stella had said the other day. Before presenting her with a half gallon of mint chocolate chip, her favorite.

Pulling her cardigan tighter around her shoulders, Marley looked out over the water now. She still hadn't found the courage to tell Owen. She'd planned on telling him the night she found out, but she'd been so exhausted from the roller coaster of emotions and the ever-present morning sickness that she'd decided on the next night. And when that night had rolled around, she'd thought the next one would be better. Before she knew it, one night had turned into two weeks.

She exhaled slowly. She'd tell him eventually, of course. Keeping it from him would be wrong. But he'd been playing so well lately, and the major-league chatter in the clubhouse had only increased since that fateful doctor's appointment. He was in the zone, pitching no-hitters nearly every week, and she couldn't seem to bring herself to drop this life-altering news just as his career was taking off.

Plus, as hard as she'd tried, she just couldn't shake the fact that he'd said he never wanted kids. She thought about it constantly—when she couldn't fall asleep at night, when she'd stare up at the ceiling with tears running into her ears, she wondered if it would be kinder for everyone just to put off telling him for a while. Until he'd been picked up by a team and had moved wherever he was destined to be. By then, she'd be showing, of course, but she could make something up if she had to. Stall until the time was right. Then they could decide together whether or not adoption was the right thing to do.

So there was that. But there was another reason why the thought of telling him was so hard... She'd been rejected by her own father. She didn't think she could take the look of regret in Owen's eyes at the thought of bringing their child into the world. She was still confused, still getting used to the idea of a baby, but she found that her mothering instinct was fierce. The need to protect this little life from any-thing that could harm it, real or hypothetical, was a force that she wouldn't be able to quell if she tried.

Looking down at the sand, she kicked at a pebble with the toe of her shoe and watched it go skipping into the water.

"What are you thinking about?" Frances asked.

She looked over to see her foster mother watching her.

The breeze blew her hair over her face, and she pushed it back with a sigh. "So many things. I can't keep them all straight."

"I get it, honey. Life just threw you a pretty big curveball."

Boy, had it ever. There were so many things she could have done differently. She could have made sure she'd had backup birth control, for one. Or she could have never slept with Owen at all. But the fact was, she'd made those choices, and those choices had brought her to this moment. As scared as she was, she couldn't wish away the baby she was carrying. And she couldn't wish away that night of passion, where she'd felt truly wanted for the first time in her life.

Yes, life had thrown her a curveball. But she was just going to have to learn how to catch them from now on.

"I just want to do what's right for all of us," she said. "But there's so much riding on the timing. It feels like I'm walking on the edge of a cliff, and if I slip, I'm going to fall."

Frances slowed beside her and then stopped.

Marley stopped, too.

"You might fall," Frances said. "But your sisters and I will be here to catch you. You know that, right?"

Marley smiled. She was so lucky to have her family. So many women had to negotiate things like this all by themselves. It happened every day, in every corner of the world. She knew how blessed she was.

"What would I do without you?" she asked.

"You're a strong girl. You'd manage."

"I'm not so sure about that."

Frances put an arm around her, and they began walking again.

"Honestly," Marley said, "I can't fathom being a mother. I don't know if I can do it. At least, not well, and I won't put a child through that."

"You had a rough childhood. It makes sense that you'd have doubts about this. But that doesn't make you any less of a mother. Sometimes the most loving, selfless thing a mother can do is entrust her child to someone else. Just remember, only you can make the best decision for you and your baby. The rest of us are here to support you, whatever path you take."

Marley swallowed down the sudden lump in her throat. She wondered what her life would've been like if her dad had made that decision early on instead of keeping her when it was obvious he didn't want her. Things would've been different, for sure. But would they have been better? After all, she'd found herself with Frances. And what could've been better than that?

An easy silence settled between them as they continued walking beside the foamy waves. Seagulls bobbed on the wind overhead, and Marley looked out to see a small fishing boat making its way past the swells. If someone had told her six months ago that she'd be back in Christmas Bay, she wouldn't have believed them. But back in Christmas Bay and *pregnant*?

Talk about a curveball.

Owen took an even breath and knocked on the door to the announcer's booth. The game had been over for an hour, and the park was nearly empty. He'd taken his time in the locker room, hoping to let the crowd clear out before he stepped outside. He hadn't wanted to be mobbed on his way to see Marley, which was beginning to be one of his favorite postgame traditions.

After home games, he'd bring her a Coke and a bag of peanuts, something she seemed to be craving lately, and they'd shoot the breeze. They'd talk about baseball, how he'd pitched that night and the things he might've done better. But more and more, they'd talk about life. Stupid things, like her new love for peanuts. And not so stupid things, like growing up with abusive fathers. Marley had become a good friend. But he still couldn't help imagining her naked. He imagined her naked a lot.

He had no idea if she imagined him naked, but it didn't matter. He was trying really hard to be a decent guy. Someone she could count on. Someone who didn't make her feel like all he cared about was getting back in her pants.

Still, when the door opened, and it wasn't her standing there, but one of the tech guys instead, his disappointment was almost palpable.

"Hey, Tony," he said. "Is Marley still around? I was hoping to catch her before she left."

"Sure, she's here. Just going over some play-by-play that she wasn't happy with."

Owen smiled. When it came to baseball, he'd always thought he was a perfectionist. But he was nothing compared to Marley, who was constantly honing her craft, working to get to that next level. And imagining problems with her delivery that just weren't there.

"Great game tonight," Tony said as Owen walked in. "When you step on that mound, we can hear a pin drop up here."

"Oh yeah?"

"True story. I'm gonna grab my stuff and head out. Will you tell her I'll see her tomorrow?"

"Sure thing."

She was sitting with her back turned to him. The room was dim, and the stadium lights outside the big windows were so bright, he could only make out her silhouette against them—hair pulled high into a ponytail, headset over her ears. Her head tilted in a way that said she was concentrating.

He pulled the Cokes and peanuts out of his jogger pockets and pulled a chair up behind her, careful not to make any noise. This close, he could smell her perfume, and his stomach tightened. He watched the way her hand gripped one of the earpieces, and he was struck again by how good at her job she was. How lucky the Sharks were to have her. And then he thought about how lucky he'd been to have her, and all of a sudden, he couldn't take his eyes off her. Just like Max had said. It was true. She was all-consuming.

After a minute, she leaned back and took her headphones off.

"Hey."

She startled and turned.

"Sorry," he said. "I didn't want to bother you, so I snuck in."

Smiling, she looked around. "Where's Tony?"

"He told me to tell you he went home."

"I see you brought my favorite thing in the whole wide world."

He set the Cokes and peanuts on the desk and leaned back in his chair to look at her. "Not sure when this started to be the best part of the day, but it totally is."

"I think that officially makes us old."

"Officially."

She cracked open the Coke and took a sip. "Mmm. That's so good. Thank you."

"You're welcome."

"Are you still on a high from that game? You have to be. You were amazing."

He swiveled back and forth in his chair. He was definitely on a high, but it wasn't all from the game. Some of it was from just being close to her. "I could get used to a beautiful woman telling me I'm amazing."

"You act like that never happens."

He winked at her. "First time today."

"You're so humble."

"Speaking of, I have some news," he said. "I wanted you to be the first to know."

She set her Coke on the desk and leaned forward, her green eyes sparkling. She always made him feel like she cared about what he had to say.

"I'm all ears," she said. "What is it?"

"Coach said the Mariners are interested in bringing me up."

Her eyes widened. "Really?"

"Really."

"Oh, Owen. That's fantastic. I'm so, so proud of you."

"It's way too early to get excited, but it's something. More than I got last year, that's for damn sure."

"I don't think it's too early to get excited. I think you should be celebrating." Her eyebrows knitted together. "Speaking of, why aren't you out with the team? I know they were grabbing a few drinks tonight…"

He shrugged. "I thought I'd ask if you wanted to grab a drink. Just us."

"Oh. Uh…I can't. I'd really love to, but I just can't."

"Why not?"

She licked her lips, looking for the most part like she didn't have a good answer to that. At least, not one she was willing to share.

"If you're worried about us picking up where we left off," he said, "you don't have to be. I've been good, right? Haven't tried to get you back into bed? I mean, I'd *like* to get you back into bed…"

She laughed. "It's not that."

"Then what?"

She took another sip of her Coke, then set it down carefully. She shifted in her chair, looking like she was trying to get comfortable. His gaze shifted to her stomach, where her hand was resting.

He frowned. "Are you sick?"

"Off and on."

"Off and on… What does that mean?"

She watched him steadily. And then his gut tightened. It felt like all the oxygen was being sucked out of the room. *The nausea over the last several weeks. The dizziness. The exhaustion…* How the hell could he have missed it? How could he have been so stupid?

All of a sudden, he was the one who felt sick.

"Marley," he said. "Are you…?"

She was quiet for a long, meaningful moment. And then she swallowed visibly. "I'm pregnant, Owen."

He leaned back, feeling like she'd just hit him with a baseball bat. With his own baseball bat. And then kicked him in the ribs for good measure.

"AJ and I didn't break up until right before I moved

back to Christmas Bay," she said. "We'd been trying to figure things out for a while… You don't have to worry, okay?"

He let that settle. There was a small voice in the back of his head that was telling him not to be too quick about this, not to be too relieved. She might've been with AJ before she'd come home, but she'd spent the night with him not long after. There were two men in the mix here, not just one.

But the temptation not to argue, to relax into his chair and not read too much into her words just now, was too great.

"Are you okay?" she asked. "Say something."

He scraped a hand through his hair. "Sorry, sorry. I'm just surprised."

"I know."

"How long have you known?"

"A few weeks."

"And you didn't tell me? Why?"

She looked out the window to the field below. Her profile was lovely.

"I needed some time," she said. "To figure it out."

He put a hand on her knee. She was wearing slacks tonight. Another one of her blouses buttoned all the way to her chin. He let his gaze fall to her stomach, and he suddenly felt so protective of her that his chest tightened.

"It's gonna be okay," he said.

"That's what Frances keeps saying. And I'm trying to believe it. But some days are harder than others."

"How do you…how do you know this baby…?"

She looked back at him and covered his hand with hers. Her skin was warm and soft. Velvety. "You don't have to worry, Owen."

He still didn't know if he should believe that. But again, the temptation to follow her lead was too much. He simply wasn't prepared to believe anything else.

"I'm going to worry about you," he said. "What are you going to do?"

"I'm going to have the baby. And then? I'm not really sure. Right now I'm just trying to take it day by day. And not throw up at work."

He frowned. She'd been working this whole time. Through morning sickness and God knew what else. She came in early and stayed late, never once letting anyone know she might not be feeling up to it.

"You're a strong woman," he said.

"I don't feel very strong. I cried myself to sleep last night." At that, her eyes filled with tears. "Sorry," she said, waving her hand in front of her face. "I'm doing it again. Pregnancy hormones."

"Hey, hey, hey. Come here." He pulled her chair close and then cradled her face in his hands. She looked so sad, it was all he could do not to kiss her. Instead, he leaned forward and kissed her forehead. Something a brother might do. Or a good friend.

"You can talk to me," he said. "I'm not going anywhere."

Tears spilled down her cheeks, and he wiped them away with his thumbs.

"I'm afraid you're going to hate me," she said.

"Why would I hate you?"

She shook her head. "I mean…get sick of me. You know. If I'm crying all the time. Who'd want to stick around for that?"

"Hey, I know I'm not the most sensitive guy in the world. And I know I can be self-centered as hell, but I'd never hate you. I love you."

Her eyes met his when he said it, and his heart almost stopped in his chest. *Love.* It just tumbled out. It wasn't exactly like telling her he was *in* love with her, but he'd never said anything close to that in his life.

But as he sat there with her tears still wet on his fingertips, he knew it was the God's honest truth. He loved her. And that was okay, because normal people loved their friends, right? It didn't mean anything other than that.

"You're such a softy," she said with a smile. "Deep down."

He shook his head. "Nope. No way."

"Deny it all you want. But you've brought me peanuts and Coke for the last two weeks straight."

"Maybe I just want someone to drink with. Symbolically."

"Uh-huh."

He let his gaze settle on her lips. On that little mole beside her mouth. A few weeks ago, he didn't think she could've gotten any prettier, but he'd been wrong. Pregnancy suited her.

"I still want to take you for a drink," he said. "A nonalcoholic one. We can celebrate the baby."

"And your news."

"My news isn't as exciting as your news."

"The majors? Your dream coming true? I think it's as exciting."

The truth was, he'd completely forgotten about baseball in the last ten minutes. And he never forgot about baseball. He thought about what Max said about there being more to life, and he wondered if he'd ever get to that point. He hoped so. He couldn't think of anything more depressing than being sixty with only his memories of the good old days to keep him company.

"So, what do you say?" he asked.

"I don't know. I'm so tired. I really need to pick up groceries. I have nothing in the fridge."

His phone dinged, and he took it out of his pocket to see a text from Max. Where are you??

He looked up at her again, and she was rubbing the back of her neck with her eyes closed. She looked more than tired. She looked exhausted.

"You know what?" he said. "We can do it another night. You go home and get some rest. Tomorrow's a day off, so you can sleep in."

"I promised Stella I'd help her in the shop for a few hours. Frances has a doctor's appointment. But I'll nap after."

He wondered if she'd told AJ about this baby yet. If she hadn't, she needed to soon. The guy lived out of state, but there were things he could be doing to help. She shouldn't be having to shoulder this alone and work full-time on top of it.

"Can I walk you to your car, at least? Help you carry your bag?"

She smiled. "It's not that heavy."

"Come on. Let me do something."

"Okay, you can carry my bag."

She handed it over, and they stood just as the stadium lights flickered off.

As she turned to grab her sweater, he put his hand on the small of her back. Then thought better of it and took it away again. Wanting to protect her, to watch over her, was something he could get used to, and that worried him. He'd never felt like this before, but he had to believe it was a phase. Something that would pass when the season was over.

She smiled up at him. "Ready?"

"Let's hit it."

## *Chapter Seven*

Owen pushed the squeaky cart down the aisle, stopping in front of the dairy freezer. Marley liked ice cream; he knew that. But he wasn't sure what kind.

Opening the door, he eyed the different flavors, the different brands. There was sugar free, dairy free, gluten free. With nuts, without nuts. He rubbed the scruff on his jaw and frowned. Vanilla was probably a safe bet. Everyone liked vanilla, didn't they?

He grabbed a half gallon and tossed it in the cart. Then grabbed another for good measure. He'd texted Max before he'd left the field earlier and said he wasn't going to make it tonight. He hadn't been able to tell him the truth, of course, that he'd decided to pick up groceries for Marley instead. So, he'd told him he was tired and heading to bed early. Then came the predictable texts back—jokes about his age, his AARP membership, his retirement home application and on and on and on. It was fine. Marley was worth it.

Looking down at the cart now, he did a quick inventory. He'd gotten her some breakfast burritos and cinnamon rolls. A few frozen pizzas for when she didn't feel like cooking. Snack foods, fruits and vegetables. And he'd stopped by the vitamin section and picked up some prenatal gummies. He had no idea what pregnant women needed in general, but this seemed like a no-brainer.

He pushed the cart toward the checkout as a teenage boy with a cracking voice announced the weekly special over the intercom. It felt like a million years since he'd been that young himself, trying to negotiate the loss of his mom, the rocky road with his dad and his dream of playing professional baseball that seemed too big to fully grasp. But he had grasped it, and he'd been so close to the majors as a twenty-year-old that he'd been able to taste it.

And then, of course, it had all come crashing down. Too much partying, too many girls. He'd spent a lot of time thinking he'd thrown it away for good, but he'd worked his ass off trying to prove himself wrong. And trying to prove anyone else who thought he couldn't do it wrong. Including his own father.

Picturing his dad, Owen gripped the cart handle tighter. His patchy beard, his condescending smile. The way he always smelled like the bar and cigarette smoke and sweat. The way his words dripped from his lips like poison. Carelessly chosen but hitting their target with chilling accuracy. *No good, lazy, stupid.* He'd said those things as easily as mentioning the weather. It had been easy for him to hate his son.

Owen swallowed hard, wondering how many people went into parenthood knowing what kind of massive responsibility it was. If most of them worried they'd screw it up. Or maybe there was some kind of expectation at the beginning, that if you were born into a cycle of abuse and neglect, you'd be able to break it with your own kid.

He just knew that as a little boy, he'd never felt loved or worthy of anything. Until baseball had shown up to save him.

He clenched his jaw as he waited in the checkout line, tumbling into the memories, into the pain, before realizing he'd even gone there. He thought about Marley's baby and wondered if it would be born to a single mother just trying to get by. If it would ever know its father at all. And he pulled in a deep breath. Maybe that was for the best. Not knowing was better than feeling unloved.

He began taking the groceries out of the cart and setting them on the conveyor belt. The checker gave him a wide smile.

"How are you doing this evening?" she said.

How was he doing? He was thinking about his

childhood, so the answer was messy. He was pissed, heartbroken, bitter, sad. Incredibly sad.

"Great," he said. "How are you?"

Marley put her toothbrush back in the cup and ran her fingers over her lips. Her favorite mint toothpaste wasn't making her sick anymore, so there was that. Overall, she'd been feeling better these last few weeks, with the morning sickness easing up more and more.

But the cravings were weird, and those were only getting stronger by the day. Like the whole peanut thing. Where had *that* come from?

She put her hands on the counter and looked at herself in the mirror. She wore a sleeveless summer nightie, something that Frances had given her the minute she'd found out she was pregnant. The white eyelet fabric was adorable, but it also made her look like she'd packed on about twenty pounds. The baby couldn't weigh more than a few ounces. Which meant the rest of that weight was sitting happily in her thighs.

Sighing, she pulled her hair into a messy bun. She'd read that her hair and nails would benefit from being pregnant, and she had to admit, her skin looked better than it ever had. She did seem to be glowing. Although, that might have more to do with her broken thermostat than any kind of maternal beauty thing she had going on.

Still, as she gave herself one last look in the mirror, she had to wonder if Owen had noticed. She knew she shouldn't care either way. He wasn't her boyfriend—far from it. But he was the person she looked most forward to seeing at work, the person she wanted to run things by, talk to, laugh with. Other than the baby, their friendship was the most unexpected thing to have come from their night together. And she coveted it. She just hoped it didn't break her heart in the long run. After all, he was leaving. And when she finally told him he was the father of her baby, he'd be furious. And could she blame him?

Frowning, she turned the bathroom light off and padded down the hallway. She'd actually been close to telling him tonight. Just letting it all out and dealing with the fallout later. But then he'd told her about the Mariners being interested in him, and she just couldn't. This was the moment he'd been waiting for his entire life, what he'd been dreaming of since he was a kid. So she'd taken a deep breath and told herself it could wait just a little longer. That he could believe the baby wasn't his for now, and hoped when the time came, he'd understand.

She put a hand on her belly, something she found she was doing more and more lately, and sat down on the couch with a sigh. She wanted to do the right thing, but the right thing seemed to be changing daily. She imagined her little baby safe and warm in her womb and wished it could be like this forever. That she could just sidestep all these decisions that would impact everyone like a bomb going off.

But as she rubbed her hand gently back and forth over her belly, she realized it had grown a little. Eventually, she'd have to make those decisions, those choices, and she'd just have to trust herself with them. But it was terrifying, and all of a sudden, she felt so alone, she wanted to cry.

Picking up the remote, she squared her shoulders. Time for a movie. Something with Sandra Bullock or Goldie Hawn in it. Something that would make her laugh and forget everything for a few precious hours.

But a knock on the front door made her jump. She looked at the clock above the mantel. A little past ten. Too late for anyone other than Frances or one of her foster sisters to be stopping by.

She set the remote down and pushed off the couch with a little grunt. She headed to the front door, pausing to look through the peephole just in case. The last thing she needed was to get murdered just as she was trying to figure out the rest of her life.

But standing on her doorstep was Owen. He was leaning toward the peephole, looking right back.

*Owen?* What in the world was he doing here? When she'd left him at the ballpark, he was on his way to meet the rest of the team at a steak house at the edge of town.

"It's me!" he said, his voice muffled through the door. "Sorry it's so late, but I brought you something."

With a slow smile, she unlocked the dead bolt and opened the door. She hadn't even thought about what she was wearing until his gaze immediately swept over her body.

Her cheeks heated. "Let me grab a robe…"

"What the hell for? You look gorgeous." He leaned down and picked up two paper bags, juggling them in his arms. "I brought you some groceries."

She gaped at him. "You brought me groceries…"

"You said your fridge was empty and you were tired…"

She stood there staring at him.

"Are you going to invite me in?" he said. "Or am I going to have to unpack these in the driveway?"

She laughed. "Come in."

He stepped past, and she caught his scent. That freshly showered smell that always made her heart flutter. He smelled so good, was such a sight for sore eyes, that she was having trouble not throwing her arms around him right then and there.

She followed him in, her gaze dropping to his butt in those joggers. How could someone look this good *and* be delivering groceries just because she'd said she was tired? It was almost too good to be true.

He set the bags down, then turned to her with a boyish grin. "I'd say I'm sorry for catching you in that nightie, but that would be a lie."

Desire curled in her belly. Her pulse pounded in her ears, reminding her that they were alone. That she was barely dressed. That he was by far the sexiest man she'd ever met in her life.

"Nobody's ever done anything like this for me before," she said quietly.

"Well, maybe they should. You're going to have a baby."

She'd almost forgotten that little detail.

His gaze dropped to her stomach, and his expression changed. Tightened. "I'm not kidding, you know. Who's going to do this with you? Who's going to get you pickles and stuff in the middle of the night?"

So far, her cravings had been limited to the peanuts, and Owen had been on top of that, bless his baseball-loving heart. But as far as anything else she might need in the coming months, she hadn't let herself think about that. If she was going to survive this emotionally, she had to be stoic. And wishing she had someone to take care of her, even just a little, wasn't going to get her anywhere.

Still, his question hit a tender spot, and she felt the slightest ache in the back of her throat. She looked away before he noticed and started unpacking the groceries. It was good to have something to do.

Owen leaned against the counter, watching her. She felt his gaze, like something warm on the back of her shoulders.

"Marley."

"Mmm?"

"That wasn't a rhetorical question," he said. "I really want to know."

She opened the freezer door and put the ice cream in. Then closed it as goose bumps popped up along her arms.

When she'd told him about the baby, she hadn't technically lied. *Technically.* She knew it was a crazy stretch, but she hadn't actually said the words *AJ is the father.* But she'd deliberately led Owen to that assumption, so it was just as bad as lying.

Still, standing there now, she didn't want to turn around and face him. She didn't want to answer his question, which would only encourage more questions and more talks about the baby. And the more they talked about it, the deeper into this lie she was going to get. And she already felt awful that she'd let it get this far.

Taking an even breath, she reminded herself that she was doing this for him. She was trying to protect his dream. What might even be his destiny. She'd tell him when the time was right. She would.

"Marley," he said again. This time softer. "Will you look at me?"

She squared her shoulders and slowly turned.

"Are you going to have help?" he asked. "From what's-his-face?"

She smiled. "From AJ?"

"That's the one."

"It's complicated."

"What's complicated about it? Either he helps or he doesn't."

Marley's stomach twisted. She *really* wanted to change the subject, but judging by the look on his face, that wasn't going to happen anytime soon.

She picked up some apple juice and put it in the fridge. "He lives so far away," she said. "But he'll do what he can."

It was weak. Really weak. But it was all she could manage at the moment.

Owen crossed his arms over his chest, making his biceps bulge underneath his T-shirt sleeves. She had to work not to stare. She remembered only too well how those arms had felt around her the night this baby was conceived. How his hands, rough and calloused from swinging a baseball bat all day long, had explored her body with such skill. Despite everything, she wished she could go back to that night, if only to feel those arms wrapped around her again.

"I'm sorry," he said, "but that doesn't inspire a whole lot of confidence. He'll do what he can?"

"That came out wrong."

"Well, have you talked about it? Are you going to keep it? Raise it together?"

A wave of heat washed over her, leaving her clammy.

Owen must have noticed, because he reached out and touched her elbow. "Are you okay?"

"Just a little queasy. It'll pass."

"Go sit down. I'll bring you something to drink. What sounds good?"

"Water is perfect. Thank you."

She walked into the living room and sat with a sigh. She could hear him opening the cabinets to find the glasses and then filling one in the sink.

And then he was walking in and sitting down beside her.

"Here," he said. "Drink up."

She took a long sip. The water felt good going down, cool and refreshing on her tongue. Then she imagined it washing the lies down, and her stomach turned all over again.

"Better?" he asked.

"Much. Thank you."

Leaning forward, she set the glass on the coffee table. Her thigh rubbed against his, and there was an immediate electricity there. She longed to touch him, to feel his sinewy muscles underneath his clothes. No matter how close she was to Owen, she always wanted to be closer. It was an inconvenient truth, like so many others ruling her life lately.

"I'm sorry if I'm pushing," he said. "Asking too many questions. But I haven't been able to stop thinking about this."

She smoothed her nightie over her thighs, trying for some perspective. He was just being sweet. This did not mean he wanted anything more. And it didn't matter if he did, anyway. She didn't. At least, she hadn't before. But it was getting harder and harder to keep convincing herself of that.

"You have every right to ask questions," she said.

He raised his eyebrows.

"I mean," she said quickly, "as my friend, of course you're going to want to talk about it. Don't be sorry. It's sweet that you care."

"I told you, I'm not sweet."

"I think you are."

"That makes me feel like I don't have the upper hand here, and I always have the upper hand."

"With women? No kidding."

"Now, that makes me sound like an ass."

"You're not an ass. You're sweet."

He smiled. "I think we're talking in circles here."

"Agreed."

His smile faded, and he reached out and brushed a strand of hair away from her face. She wanted to melt into his side. She longed for more. How had she gotten herself into this? Why had she painted herself into such a corner? She'd finally found this warm, sexy, funny guy, only to keep him at arm's length. But she knew why. Because of her stupid rules. Always the rules to keep her safe and unhurt, and untouched.

"What's weird," he said, his voice low, "is that I don't want to leave you tonight. And that doesn't make any sense, because we're supposed to be friends. But friends don't necessarily want to take other friends' nighties off with their teeth."

She laughed softly. He'd teased her plenty since that night, and she'd always wondered if he wanted more, too. Sitting here now, she saw there was an undeniable heat in his eyes. It was a wonderful thing to want and be wanted. Marley thought she could live happily in this moment forever, if it weren't for the complications that came with it. He wasn't going to stay in Christmas Bay; he had much bigger fish to fry. She wasn't the settling-down type; she didn't trust anyone enough to try. And her career... She couldn't forget about her career. She'd worked just as hard and just as long as Owen had for his.

"Do you ever think about us?" he asked, leaning a little closer. She could see the flecks of green in his eyes and how, mixed with the blue, they were the color of Caribbean water.

She licked her lips. *Do you ever think about us?* The answer was yes. All the time. But telling him that felt dangerous. He absolutely didn't need to know what lay in her heart. If he did, he could use it against her someday, and Marley was all about self-preservation. She remembered the day her dad left, and she vowed never to give that much power to anyone ever again.

"I think about us," she said. "It's hard not to. We had an amazing night together."

He watched her.

"But I also think about what we decided then, too. And the reasons for deciding it."

"Refresh my memory."

She brought her feet up underneath her and pulled a pillow into her lap. With him sitting right next to her, the town house felt cozier than it ever had. The couch felt softer, the air even felt gentler against her skin. Which was ridiculous, of course. Those things were the same as they'd been twenty minutes ago. But that was how he made her feel.

"My job," she said. "Your job. We're not in a relationship kind of place... Is it coming back now?"

He ran his fingertips over her bare shoulder. "Bits and pieces."

She smiled.

"I guess you're right," he said. "But if you ever decide you want some meaningless sex, think of me."

"You're first on my list."

"As long as I'm ahead of your ex-boyfriend. I don't think I could take that."

"He's not that bad."

"He's your ex, which means I have to hate him by default."

"He's a good guy."

"If he's so great, then where the hell is he?"

Poor AJ. He was getting thrown under the bus and didn't even know it.

"He's coming in a few weeks," she said.

Owen's expression tightened. "Well, that's good. I'm glad he's making it a priority."

"He couldn't get off work, or he would've been here sooner. It's not his fault."

"Sounds like you're making excuses for him. If it were me—"

He stopped short and looked away. She could feel her heart beating in her throat. *If it were him, what?*

Outside, the wind blew against the windows, rattling them. But other than that, the silence between them was heavy. She pinched the edge of the pillow between her fingertips and watched him. The muscles in his jaw were working, and there was a distinct tilt to his head. Like he was deciding whether or not to say something.

He looked back at her. "Are you sure it's not mine?" he asked. "I mean, I can't help but wonder. The timing..."

She reached for his hand and squeezed it. God, she hated this. She hated lying to him, but now she was going to have to. Straight up. She just hoped she was doing it for the right reasons, and not because she was terrified of his rejection. That he'd turn out to be just like her dad and leave before she could ever love him properly. And then there was the baby. The sweet little baby who hadn't asked for any of this but who would be living with the consequences its entire life.

She'd never been much of a praying person, but she seemed to be doing a lot of it lately. She took a breath and asked for strength as he watched her expectantly. She thought she could see a sliver of fear in his eyes. Fear that she was going to tell him the baby was his?

And then, miraculously, those familiar walls rose around her heart. Just when she needed them most. They would protect her. And they would give her the courage to say what she needed to, until the time was right. Until he was playing in the majors, and she was over him. Then she could come clean, and he could hate her, justifiably, but at least she'd have given him the time he needed.

"It's not yours," she said, forcing a steadiness into her voice that she didn't feel. "Please don't worry about this."

After a second, his expression relaxed a little. And she knew she'd done the right thing. He was relieved.

"Well, I'm just saying," he said. "He should be here with you. Job or no job. You shouldn't be doing this alone."

"I'm not alone. I have Frances and Stella and Kyla. And I have you."

He reached out and pulled her into a hug then. She went willingly, laying her head against his warm, solid chest, where she could feel his heart beating against her cheek.

"I know we don't know each other very well, Marley," he said. "But I feel like we do. Does that make sense?"

She closed her eyes when they started to sting. She didn't want to cry, but she didn't think she'd be able to help it if he kept up like this. She hadn't known how much she'd needed this hug until he'd pulled her into it. She turned her face into his shirt, where it smelled like fabric softener, deodorant and Owen.

"It makes perfect sense," she said.

He kissed the top of her head. She could feel the warmth of his breath there and the softness of his mouth, and her heart broke, even as she begged it not to. The truth was, he was going to leave. And that was okay, because he had an amazing gift. And she was going to be happy for him when he went. Because even though they didn't know each other very well, she also knew she loved him anyway. She just did.

They sat there curled into each other as the wind blew outside. She imagined Frances's lovely old house on the cape, standing there like it had for the last century overlooking the blustery ocean. And she wondered how many things could stand the test of time like that. That were strong enough to hold up through storms and uncertainty, and the forces of nature that were beyond control. And she wondered if love might be one of those things.

She'd never considered it before. But tonight, as she sat there listening to the steady beat of Owen's heart, she was considering it now.

## Chapter Eight

Marley bit her lip and hung up the phone. Dr. Binky's on-call nurse didn't think it was anything to worry about. Spotting in the first trimester didn't necessarily mean anything was wrong, but she wanted Marley to go to the hospital just in case.

She looked up at the clock. Midnight. Urgent care closed at eight, so the ER was her only choice. It sounded scarier than it was. At least, that was what she kept telling herself as she forced in another shaky breath.

Outside, the wind from earlier had turned stronger, more insistent. And now the first drops of rain began pelting the windows, promising a full-fledged storm.

She swung her legs over the side of the bed and looked for her slippers. But when she tried standing up, she felt a warm stickiness between her thighs. She sank down on the bed again, light-headed. She was so worried, so scared, she wasn't sure she'd be able to stand up again, much less manage to walk in a straight line.

Dropping a hand to her stomach, she took another breath. Then another. In through her nose, out through her mouth. "It's okay, baby," she whispered. "Everything's going to be okay. Just hang on, all right?"

Sitting there cradling her belly, she felt a rush of love so strong that it rivaled the dizziness in her head. There was no doubt this pregnancy had thrown her for a loop. And if she could've planned it for a different time in her life, she would have. But now that this baby was here, she'd been wondering if it was a boy or a girl. What it would look like, if it would have Owen's eyes or her lips. She wondered what it would feel like to hold it for the first time, wondering if she would have the strength to give it up. Even to someone who would love it unconditionally. All these things had been swirling around in her brain and heart, and now, the possibility of losing it terrified her.

She looked at the phone on the nightstand, knowing she needed to call someone. She didn't want to drive when she was this shaky. But Frances was out of the question. Marley knew she'd be beside herself if she got a call at midnight asking for a ride to the hospital, even if it was only a precaution. And Kyla was out of town with Ben and his little girl. They'd taken her to the zoo in Portland. Which left Stella, and she was the deepest sleeper Marley knew. She'd have to call the landline at Frances's house, and that would wake them both up.

Closing her eyes for a second, she focused on her breathing. *In...out...* There *was* one more person she could call, and she knew he'd be there in a heartbeat. It was only last night that Owen had told her he wanted to be there for her. Under any other circumstance, she'd just tuck that away as something sweet he said. But right then, she did need him. And she'd picked up the phone and was dialing his number before she could talk herself out of it.

It only rang once before he picked up, sounding groggy. "Marley," he said. "What's wrong?"

"I'm so sorry to be calling like this, but I need a ride to the hospital, and—"

*"What?"* he said quickly, panic slipping into his tone. "Are you okay?"

"I'm okay, I'm all right, but I woke up spotting a little, and I called the nurse, and she wants me to get checked out just in case. I didn't want to call Frances, she'd probably have an accident getting here in this weather, and Kyla is out of town, and—"

"I'm on my way," he said, cutting her off. "Just sit tight. I'll be there in two minutes."

His voice was so warm and reassuring that she immediately choked up.

"Thank you, Owen."

"I'm just glad you called," he said. "It's going to be okay. Try not to worry. I'll be there soon."

And then he hung up, and she lowered the phone from her ear, feeling numb. She needed to get some clothes on. She couldn't leave the house in her nightgown.

After a second, she stood, her legs wobbly underneath her. Then she grabbed a new pair of underwear from her nightstand and joggers and a T-shirt from her closet.

She threw her clothes on, and headed for the front door just as a pair of headlights shone through the rain-beaded window. He was here. For some reason, a deep calm settled over her then. Whether it made any sense or not, she suddenly felt safe.

She grabbed her purse and opened the front door.

Owen was headed up the walkway in the rain, his eyes puffy underneath his baseball cap.

Stepping forward, he pulled her into a hug.

"It's okay," he said into her hair. "Don't worry."

And then he was guiding her toward his truck that sat running at the curb, its windshield wipers swooshing back and forth.

He opened the passenger-side door and she climbed in, holding her stomach protectively. She kept reminding herself what the nurse said. *Fairly common, probably nothing to worry about, come in just to make sure...* She repeated the words in her head over and over again as they made their way to the hospital. The road rose and fell along the cliffs of Cape Longing, with the ocean dark and brooding below. On a sunny day, the forest to their left was whimsical and green, but now looked like something waiting to gobble them up if they made the mistake of turning into it. The rain was coming in sheets now, and Owen was having to lean forward to see out the windshield.

Marley looked out the window, glad she hadn't called Frances. This weather was scary.

Owen put a hand on her leg. "Almost there," he said. "How are you doing?"

"Just thinking."

"About?"

"How grateful I am that I had you to call."

"I meant what I said, Marley."

She glanced over at him, and his profile looked stern in the gritty light of the truck's cab. "You shouldn't be doing this alone," he continued. "AJ needs to get his ass out here."

"He will."

"You keep saying that, but I'm starting to wonder if it's true."

Her stomach dropped. She tried to think of an appropriate response, but then the hospital came into view. *Saved by the bell.* She'd never been so happy to see a hospital in her life.

"Why don't you just drop me off out front," she said, "and then you can park?"

Nodding, he pulled up to the sliding glass doors

and came to a stop. "Can you get there okay? Are you hurting?"

"I'm all right. I'll see you inside." She gave him what she hoped was a reassuring smile. "Thanks."

She headed toward the doors as he pulled away with a screech of his tires. There was definitely a slight ache in her lower belly now.

*It's okay, baby*, she thought. *Just hold on...*

Marley sat on the examining room table, waiting for the doctor. She shifted nervously, and the tissue paper crinkled underneath her. She could hear voices coming from down the hallway and held her breath for a minute, listening.

"Excuse me? Sir?" a woman asked.

"Yeah." *Owen's voice.* And the sound of it soothed her. Like a warm blanket in a chilled room.

"Hi," he said. "I'm looking for my friend. About this tall, cute, blonde. Pregnant lady..."

"Oh, yes. They just brought her back. She said you'd be coming in. She's down the hall, exam room two."

"Thank you."

Marley scooted off the bed and padded over to the slide-away curtain, poking her head through.

Owen was standing a few yards away, looking at the numbers above the rooms. The hospital didn't seem that big from the outside, but inside it was surprisingly huge. Everything she'd heard about its emergency department had been overwhelmingly positive, including the fact that one of their outfielders had gotten stitches here recently when he'd taken a grounder to the head, and he'd lived. So that was what she was trying to concentrate on now as she waved Owen over.

"Hey, you," she said. "In here."

When he saw her, he smiled and looked down at her feet. "Nice socks."

"I know. They've got the fancy grippers on the bottom, and the gown doesn't close in the back, so I'm all set in my hospital attire. Come in."

"Are you sure they're going to let me stay?" he asked, brushing past.

She climbed back up on the bed again and arranged the gown over her thighs. "I don't think they'd be able to turn away Christmas Bay's answer to Nolan Ryan. Not when it comes right down to it."

"I don't know about Nolan *Ryan*, but I'll take it." He sat in a plastic chair opposite her, and it squeaked under his weight. "How are you feeling?"

"I stopped bleeding, so that's a good sign. The nurse told me that someone with a broken arm just came in, so I'll need to wait a little longer, but they don't seem too worried. They said bleeding can be common this early on. They'll do an ultrasound and an exam, and if everything looks normal, I can go home."

"I don't think you should stay by yourself tonight."

"I'm okay. The seagulls keep me company." She'd

meant for that to be lighthearted, but it came out sounding depressing.

He noticed. The muscles in his jaw bunched and relaxed. And then he shook his head. "Nope. I'm staying over. I can crash on your couch."

"You don't have to do that."

"I want to. Please don't make me beg."

Her heart squeezed. "I'd never make you beg. You can sleep over anytime."

"Anytime? Maybe we can graduate from the couch to your bed?"

The teasing felt good. It felt right. It was so nice to have him here, distracting her and keeping her talking. Keeping her thoughts from turning scary and dark.

"Have I ever told you how gorgeous you look in a hospital gown?" he asked.

"You've never seen me in a hospital gown."

"Well, you should wear them more often."

"I look like a house."

"You look like a bombshell."

"That's hard to believe."

"You have no idea how beautiful you are."

She felt herself blush. Her father used to tell her she was fat. So, no. Her self-image wasn't her strong suit. But when she saw herself through Owen's eyes, she looked very different. She looked like a woman whose curves might be sexy, not shameful. It was just one of the many, many things she was coming to love about him. How he made her feel.

"Being pregnant has already changed my body so much," she said quietly. "But I actually like it. I didn't expect that."

"Why wouldn't you? It's an amazing thing. You're sustaining life in there."

It was a lovely thing to say, and she had to agree. The female body was capable of so much. It was a wonder in and of itself.

"You know," he said, "I have a feeling this kid is going to be an athlete."

Marley ran her hands down her thighs. The chances of that were pretty good, considering its father was Owen Taylor. The pitcher who had a major-league team taking a closer look. But of course, she couldn't say that. She shouldn't even be thinking it, in case he could read it all over her face.

"Oh yeah?" she said, looking down. "How do you know?"

"I just know. I can feel it."

It was possible there was already a bond between him and his child. She'd had a sad experience with her own dad, but that didn't mean strong natural bonds didn't exist, even before birth. And again, she felt sick that she hadn't told him the truth yet. The longer this went on, every hour that passed, she was digging herself deeper and deeper.

She clasped her hands in her lap. She'd tell him soon. As soon as he had an offer on the table, she'd say something. And then she'd try and make leaving Christmas Bay as easy as she could for him.

"Marley?"

She and Owen turned at the same time to see a woman in a white lab coat pulling the curtain open.

"Yes, hi."

"I'm Dr. Marksberry. I hear you've been having some bleeding tonight?"

"A little, but it's stopped now." She could hear the hopefulness in her own voice. *Please let it be stopped...*

The doctor nodded and stepped up to the computer stand by the wall. She began typing busily but turned to give Marley a smile over her shoulder. "This can happen in early pregnancy as your body adjusts to the hormones and everything else going on in there. The fact that you're not cramping is very good and that you're not bleeding heavily. It's probably nothing to worry about, but I'm glad you came in. It's always better to be safe than sorry in these situations."

She turned to Owen. "And who's this?"

"Oh, I'm sorry," Marley said. "This is the—" She caught herself before she said *the baby's father*. Oh, God. What a mess she'd created for herself. "This is the friend who gave me a ride."

The doctor reached out and shook his hand. "Nice to meet you, Owen. I'm hoping to have you two out the door soon. We'll just do a quick exam and ultrasound, and you'll be able to go home and get some sleep, Marley. How does that sound?"

"Thanks, Doc," Owen said. Then he leaned forward and took Marley's hand.

She held on tight. And wondered when the time came, how she'd ever be able to let go.

Owen guided Marley up her walkway with his arm around her shoulders. He was trying to protect her from the worst of the rain, which was coming in sideways now, but it wasn't much use. They were getting soaked anyway.

When they reached the front door, she dug her keys out of her pocket and unlocked the dead bolt. Then she stepped inside with him right behind her.

She flipped on the lights and shook her hair out. He could smell her shampoo from where he stood, and his groin tightened. When he'd offered to stay the night, he truly hadn't been thinking of anything other than supporting her, no matter how much he joked otherwise.

But now, standing there in her foyer, with the wind howling outside and the scent of rain in the air, he wondered if he'd have the strength to keep from kissing her again. From pulling her close, which was what he'd been wanting to do for weeks now. But then he felt guilty about that. She was so tired, so worn out from her scare tonight. He really didn't know what to do with himself.

She hung her purse over a chair and put her hands on the small of her back with a sigh. The thin, damp fabric of her T-shirt stretched across her full breasts and swollen stomach. If he didn't know she was pregnant, he wouldn't have thought anything of it. He would've thought she was just naturally soft, curvaceous. But he did know, and his gaze lingered there for a long moment. And something in his heart stirred. She'd be an amazing mother if she decided to keep this baby. She was such a sweet, loving person, who deserved all the good things. He just hoped she wouldn't have to do this alone. And again, there was a flash of anger toward her douchey ex-boyfriend who was two thousand miles away at that very moment.

Turning to him with a smile, she tucked her hair behind her ears. "Let's see… I need to get you a blanket and a pillow. I still feel bad that I woke you up in the middle of the night like this. And you have an away game tomorrow…"

"Not too far away. Only a few hours, and I can use the drive to catch up on my needlepoint."

"Right."

"You think these hands only know their way around baseball bats? There's more to me than meets the eye."

"I don't doubt that," she said. "I just don't think it's needlepoint."

"You're gonna have to eat crow when I give you your monogrammed napkins for Christmas."

"I don't think you're going to be here at Christmas, Owen."

She said this casually while kicking her tennis shoes off, but the words settled heavily in the air anyway. He was surprised at the way they made him feel—melancholic, sad. If he wasn't here at Christmas, that meant he'd been picked up by a team, and that was a very good thing.

He shoved that thought aside and walked over to her. She was rubbing her neck, looking tired. The doctor at the hospital had confirmed the bleeding was nothing to worry about but had said to come right back if anything changed. Right now, she just looked exhausted from the scare. And from being pregnant in general.

"I'm still making you those monogrammed napkins," he said. "Because everyone needs monogrammed napkins. It's the law."

She smiled, fixing him with that seafoam gaze. There were dark smudges underneath her eyes. "For all the fancy parties I throw?"

"Who knows? By then, you might be a famous announcer, schmoozing with all the baseball big shots."

"In Christmas Bay?"

"You're schmoozing with me, aren't you? Christmas Bay's answer to Nolan Ryan."

"Ah. I stand corrected." She winced suddenly and touched her neck.

"What's wrong?"

"Nothing. Just a cramp. Too much tension, I guess."

"Come here." He held out his hand. "I'm going to give you a massage before bed."

"Owen. You've got to sleep. You're going to be worn out tomorrow."

"Baby, if I told you how little sleep I used to get in the good old days, you wouldn't believe it. And I still played ball."

"But you're not twenty-one anymore, either."

"Ouch."

"I'm just saying—"

"You're just saying I'm only getting better with age."

"I wouldn't argue with that."

"So, you think I'm hot?"

Her cheeks colored. "I wouldn't argue with that, either."

"Well, now. See? I've got you right where I want you."

"And where's that?"

"About to be getting a massage." He hooked his finger at her. "Come here."

She watched him for a long, charged moment. For a second, he thought she might turn him down cold. Break his heart, walk into her bedroom and close the door behind her.

But then she smiled and stepped forward to put her hand in his.

He looked down at her, wondering how in God's

name he hadn't noticed her all those years ago. When they were in high school together and had been free to do whatever they wanted. He wished he could go back in time and hold out his hand to her at seventeen. He wondered if he'd been kinder to her, if he'd seen her for who she really was, if she would've taken it then. He wondered how his life might have turned out if he'd met Marley earlier.

But he was here with her now, with her fingers wrapped around his, with a storm raging outside, and her scent lingering in the air. No matter what happened from this moment on, he knew that, tonight, he was a lucky man.

He led her over to the couch, where he sat down. She sat, too, her thigh brushing against his.

Gently, he took her by the shoulders and turned her so she was facing away. Her hair fell in beachy waves, tickling the backs of his hands as he put them on either side of her neck.

He'd had so many body aches and muscle cramps over the years that he knew how to give a pretty killer massage by now. He squeezed her trapezius muscle between his thumb and fingers until she moaned.

"Does that hurt?"

"No," she said. "Keep going."

"I just want you to know that I'm going to be mature here and not read too much into that."

Smiling, she leaned her head to the side as he began moving his thumbs in a gentle circle. Then went back to the area closest to her neck and moved outward again, until he felt her relax into him. Her skin was warm and soft, and he couldn't help imagining lifting her shirt over her head and working his hands over her bare back. But he was trying to be good, he really was. And if she were half naked, there was no telling where this might end up. When it came right down to it, he'd make a terrible masseuse.

"Where did you learn to do this?" she asked, turning to look at him over her shoulder.

"Injuries and therapy. Lots and lots of therapy."

"You're good at it."

"I'm good because it's you. You're not exactly hard to massage. And this is the first time I've volunteered my services for anyone, so I wouldn't know how good I am anyway."

"Ah. So, I'm special."

"You're very special."

She reached up and grabbed his hand, sitting still for a long minute. Then turned around to face him, and there were tears in her eyes.

He frowned. "What's wrong? Did I hurt you?"

"No, no. You're perfect. I'm not sure how I ever thought you weren't."

"Marley, I was an asshole. This is widely agreed upon, remember?"

"Maybe. But maybe you were just a kid who was struggling at home, like I was struggling at home. And I just wish…I just wish…"

The tears balanced on her lower lashes and then spilled down her cheeks. She didn't bother wiping them away. So he reached up and brushed his thumbs across her cheekbones.

"You just wish what, honey?"

Her face crumpled then, and he pulled her into a hug.

"This would be so much easier if you weren't so good to me," she said against his chest.

"What would be easier?"

She was quiet for a minute, her shoulders trembling. He rubbed her back in slow circles. Maybe she just needed to cry. He'd never been pregnant before, but he couldn't imagine it'd be easy on the emotions. Or the body, for that matter. Just look at what she'd gone through tonight.

He blinked, looking out the window to the darkness beyond. The rain was hitting the glass, sounding like sand blowing against it. His eyes suddenly felt gritty and heavy, but he'd sit here for the rest of the night if that was what she needed. Holding her was turning out to be one of the most natural things he'd ever done. Her head fit against the hollow below his shoulder like it was meant to go there.

Slowly, she pushed away and wiped her face with the hem of her T-shirt. Then took a deep breath, like she was getting ready to say something. A gust of wind blew against the window and rattled it. He could feel his heart beating, keeping time in his chest like a clock ticking off the seconds. And he waited.

Finally, she shook her head. "Nothing," she said. "Nothing."

## Chapter Nine

"Good evening, everyone, and welcome to another night of Tiger Sharks baseball!" Marley leaned into her mic and looked out the window overlooking the field as the crowd cheered. "Remember, tonight is seniors' night. Any fan fifty-five or over is welcome to a free soda and a medium popcorn at our concession stand."

The sun was low in the sky, sinking toward the ocean in the distance like a baseball on fire. It was warm tonight, and the announcer's box was stuffy. The stadium lights burned bright, illuminating the people in the stands like they were onstage. But the real star of the show was Owen. It seemed that with every consecutive game, the crowds got bigger and bigger as word spread about number twenty-eight, the local pitcher with the incredible arm.

Marley couldn't blame them. He was fun to watch. And for the ladies, he was more than just a talented baseball player with an impressive strikeout record— he was also eye candy. Owen was almost as popular for the way he looked as for the way he played.

But tonight, she was having a hard time concentrating on any of it, which was a rarity for her. Her mind kept wandering to AJ's phone call earlier. He was coming the day after tomorrow. It would be a quick trip, but he wanted to "talk." Something she was dreading. Not only did she need to make it clear that she wasn't interested in getting back together, but she also needed to deal with the major guilt she was feeling for making Owen think AJ was the father of her baby. *Good grief.*

She took a quick drink of water as "Walking on Sunshine," by Katrina and the Waves, began playing over the loudspeakers. Her gaze shifted to Owen, where he was warming up on deck. His stark white uniform practically glowed as he sliced his bat through the air. His jersey stretched over his powerful shoulders, his muscles straining underneath the fabric. His helmet was pulled low over his eyes, concealing them and making him seem steely and dark.

But she knew him well enough by now that she recognized this was his baseball persona—something he cultivated for his fans. Underneath, he wasn't dark at all. He was full of light and sweetness and love. At least, that was what she'd come to see over the last few weeks. Something that made her heart thrum inside her chest.

As the music faded, she leaned toward the mic again, willing herself to get her head in the game.

"And now, here's the starting lineup for tonight's game…"

She read the list of players and their positions for the visiting team from Washington. And when she got to the Tiger Sharks players, the crowd went nuts. They stomped their feet and waved their hats in the air. The night was full of electricity, and Marley could feel it to her core.

Behind her, Tony let out a soft whistle and patted her on the back. Evenings like this were exciting. It was why they were all there—the guys on the field, the coaches in the dugout, the announcers and communications team in the box. It was all for the love of baseball.

"Pitching tonight, and coming off *another* no-hitter," Marley said into the mic, "number twenty-eight, Owen Taylor!"

The crowd went bananas. Most of them got to their feet, giving him a standing ovation before he'd even stepped on the mound. Marley smiled. Not bad for his first five minutes on the job.

She continued reading off the players and their positions with a warm feeling in the pit of her stomach. She'd dreamed of this her entire life. When she'd gone to the games as an awkward preteen with holes in the toes of her Keds, she'd sit in the stands and look up at the announcer's box, imagining what it would be like up there. Safe and secure, with nothing to worry about but calling a baseball game on a balmy summer evening.

Now that she was here, her lips so close to the mic she was almost kissing it, she realized it was just as wonderful as she'd pictured. But it wasn't necessarily perfect. She'd never imagined falling in love with a player. Or worse, getting pregnant by one and having to figure out what her life was going to look like afterward. Somehow, that kind of stark reality had never crept into her fuzzy baseball dreamworld.

"Now, folks," she said, adjusting her earpiece, "I'd like to direct your attention to center field, where we have Mike Mahanay from the Hampton Opera Center in Portland singing our national anthem."

The players took off their hats, and the crowd grew quiet as the man on the field began singing one of the most beautiful versions of the anthem that she'd ever heard. Chills marched up her arms as she sat there soaking in the moment. The sights, the sounds, the smells of the ballpark. She tried to remember what it felt like to be that little girl whose home life was so sad but who took such solace in this game.

She looked up at the flag waving over the scoreboard and thought how lucky she was. If she hadn't had the father she'd had, she might never have discovered baseball. And if she'd never discovered baseball, she'd never have met Owen. And if she'd never met Owen, well...

She put a hand on her stomach. Life had a funny way of working out sometimes.


"And you're just now telling me?" AJ asked solemnly.

She watched him from across the table at the little Mexican restaurant overlooking the bay. It was small, quiet. She'd thought it would be a good place to talk.

But sitting here now, seeing the look of disappointment unfold across his face, she wished she'd just told him at home. At home, she could at least be sitting with her feet up. And maybe with a cold cloth on her forehead for good measure. A little dramatic, sure. But she was pregnant, so she felt like she was allowed.

She took a long sip of her soda, savoring the fizzy sweet taste. It was also a way to postpone having to answer him, at least for a second or two.

Setting the soda down again, she put her hands on the table. As if to keep it from flying away.

"I'm sorry," she said softly. "I just didn't know how."

"How about picking up the phone and calling me?

I mean, we have good communication, right? Or I always thought we did."

"Of course we do. And I should've. But it's harder than you think, believe me."

He sighed, running his fingers over the rim of his beer mug. "I know. I know it must be. I just want you to know that I'm here for you. Even though you won't consider coming back to me. And are totally breaking my heart, by the way."

He said this with a small smile, but she could see there was real pain underneath the surface. At least she'd told him. At least she'd been open about that part and wasn't stringing him along. She didn't think she could say one more thing that wasn't the complete truth, no matter what the subject. It took too much of a toll. It was too hard to reconcile all these things in her heart.

"I'll always love you," she said, reaching out to hold his hand. "You know that, right?"

"I know." He squeezed her fingers. "But from here on out, you have to act like it. Tell me when significant things are happening in your life. Like, I don't know. Pregnancy, maybe?"

She smiled. "Deal."

The waiter came and brought more chips and salsa. Then left them alone again in the dim restaurant.

AJ leaned back in his chair and scrubbed a hand through his short brown hair. "So, what are you going to do, Marley? Does this guy know?"

Nibbling on a chip, she shook her head. "No. Not yet. I've been waiting for the right time."

"And when is that?"

"When he gets picked up by the majors. It's going to happen anytime now, and that way he won't be tempted to stay out of guilt. He's got to go where his job is. Where the money is."

"What about your job?"

"I could have a baby and call games at the same time."

"It'd be harder, though. A lot harder."

"It would be, but I also wouldn't be reinventing the wheel, either. Women raise babies by themselves all the time."

He nodded, taking a sip of his beer.

Marley looked over as the door across the restaurant opened with a swoosh of salty sea air. And Owen walked in.

Her heart stopped. He was with a group of guys—Max and a couple of the assistant coaches. It wasn't until right then that she remembered him saying he liked this place once. That it had the best fajitas he'd ever eaten. That he came here after games sometimes… *Why* hadn't she remembered that earlier?

"What?" AJ twisted around and followed her gaze.

"Oh, God," she said. "He's here."

"Who's here?"

*"Him."*

And as soon as she said it, Owen looked right at her.

"*Him*, him?" AJ asked.

There wasn't time to say anything else, because he began making his way toward them with his jaw set. Definitely set. She could see the muscles working from where she sat.

He stopped at their table and looked down at her. "Hey," he said, his voice even. And then his gaze shifted to AJ. And that was when she recognized the pissed look on his face. Definitely pissed. "Is this who I think it is?"

Marley thought she could feel her heart pounding against her spine. It was possible that she'd underestimated how protective Owen felt over her. Because his neck was red above his collar. His ears were even red.

She sat forward and cleared her throat. "Owen, this is AJ. He's here all the way from Iowa..."

AJ reached out his hand, and Owen shook it firmly. All Marley could do was pray that neither one of them would mention the baby.

Someone upstairs must have been listening, because after a second, Owen gave AJ a thin smile. It wasn't his most charming, but it was something. And she relaxed a fraction.

"Nice to meet you."

"You, too," AJ said. "I hear you've got a wicked arm. I've got to head out tomorrow, or I'd come see you play."

Owen nodded. "That's too bad. I'm sure Marley would like you to stay longer. It'd be nice for her to have your support."

Marley's stomach dropped. *Uh-oh.*

AJ looked up at him curiously.

"Uh, he's got to get back for work," she said quickly, "or I'm sure he'd want to stay longer. I haven't had a chance to show him around Christmas Bay yet. Have I, AJ?"

Her pulse was racing now. This was a nightmare. What were the odds that Owen would walk into the same place she and AJ were having dinner, on the exact same night? Actually, they were pretty good, according to Murphy's Law.

"Yeah," AJ said. "I'd love to stay. But I'll be back. I have some time off coming this Christmas."

Owen raised his eyebrows. "This *Christmas*?"

AJ glanced at Marley, confused.

She smiled. *Oh, God.* Maybe she deserved this. It was her punishment for not coming clean with Owen to begin with. Frances always used to say that fibs, even ones told to protect someone else, would always come back to bite you in the end. And now look where she was. Bitten and then some.

"Yeah," AJ said, looking back up at Owen. "I'll be back at Christmas. Why?"

"Nothing. It just seems like quite a while for Marley to be on her own like this."

"Like this..."

"Owen!" Max called from their booth across the room. "We're ordering, bro."

Owen waved from over his shoulder. "Coming."

And all of a sudden, Marley couldn't tell what he was thinking anymore. His expression was shuttered.

"You two have a nice dinner," he said tightly. "See you tomorrow, Marley."

"See you tomorrow."

And then he was walking away, leaving her struggling for a normal breath.

AJ shook his head, watching him go. "Wow. He's intense."

"He's just worried about me."

"He's in love with you."

"No. No, he's not."

AJ looked back at her. "Really? It's pretty obvious, Marley."

She was having trouble processing that. All of a sudden, she had a pounding headache and was so exhausted that she slumped back in her chair. "I'm sorry," she said. "About all that. I was going to wait to tell him, but maybe that's not the right thing. It feels so complicated."

"Well, he should know. I can tell you that much."

She rubbed her temple.

"You think he'll be mad?" AJ asked.

"Probably. But that's not what I'm worried about most. I'm worried he won't care at all. I mean, I don't think that's Owen. But there's a part of me, ever since my dad, that doesn't believe…" She let her voice trail off. It was getting too painful. Too much to bear, sitting here in this restaurant in front of a man who was struggling with his own pain. She was just tired of pain. She'd felt enough of it to last a lifetime.

"Hey," AJ said.

She looked at him.

"Whatever happens, I'm here. Even if I'm not *here*. Even if I'm back home, you can call me anytime, and we can talk it out, okay?"

She gave him a weary smile. "What did I ever do to deserve you?"

"I think it's the other way around. We were great together, even if we couldn't go the distance. But I'll be happy being your friend, too. Just as long as I get to be part of your life."

"You'll always be part of my life, AJ."

He watched her from across the table, his brown eyes warm, if a little sad. "Are you ready to order?"

"I'm ready," she said. But she didn't think she could eat if she tried.


Owen peeled his T-shirt off and threw it in the corner. He was bone tired. They'd won tonight's game, but they'd had to work for it. He hadn't played as well as he should've, and that bothered him.

But what really had him unsettled was seeing Marley and her ex at Garcia's afterward. He hadn't been able to hide his disdain very well. But who could blame him? As far as he was concerned, the guy was already an absentee father. *He'd be back at Christmas*... What the hell? By then the baby would be here already.

He sat on the edge of his bed and put his head in his hands. He just hadn't expected to feel this way about Marley. If he was going to make it out of Christmas Bay and into the majors, he needed to start concentrating on the game, not whether or not the father of her kid was visiting enough.

She was his friend. But that was as far as it went. He had to keep reminding himself of that, period.

His phone dinged from the dresser, and he leaned over to pick it up.

There was a text from Marley across the screen, and he swiped it open.

Are you awake?

He stared at it for a second. It was past midnight. He never heard from her this late.

Are you okay? he texted back.

Just need to talk for a minute. I don't think it can wait.

Call me.

I'm actually outside. Can I come in?

He felt a prickle of heat across his chest. Maybe she'd gotten into it with AJ. Maybe she wanted to get back together with him and needed advice. Was he in a position to advise her on what she should do about another guy? He knew the answer to that.

Getting up, he grabbed his T-shirt from the floor. Then he headed down the hallway to the front door.

When he opened it, she was standing on the doorstep chewing on her bottom lip.

"What's wrong?" he asked. "What's going on?"

She stared up at him, and he thought her eyes looked red-rimmed. Like maybe she'd been crying.

"I'm sorry," she said. "I don't want to worry you, and everything is okay… I mean, it's not okay. But I'm fine." She swallowed visibly. "Can I come in?"

He led her inside and pulled out a chair at the kitchen table. It was messy, as usual. He really needed to start picking things up like a grown-ass adult.

He cleared some junk mail away, keeping an eye on her the whole time.

"You look like you've seen a ghost," he said. "Are you sure you're all right?"

She gave him a wobbly smile. "Do you have something fizzy to drink? It settles my stomach."

He opened the cupboard, got a glass out and filled it with Diet Coke. Then he sat down beside her and handed it over.

"Thanks," she said.

"You're worrying me. Just tell me what's going

on. Does this have anything to do with AJ? Am I going to have to go beat his ass?"

She took a sip, then touched her fingers to the corner of her mouth. Her hand was shaking.

"God, no. Don't do that."

"Then what?"

She took a breath, and that was shaky, too. Then she locked gazes with him, and there was something in her eyes that told him this wasn't just any late-night visit because of a fight with an ex. This was something more. Something much more, and his gut tightened.

"I've got something to tell you." Closing her eyes for a second, she shook her head. "I don't even know where to start…"

"Did you hit my truck or something?" It was a pathetic attempt at humor, but the moment felt awkward and heavy. His palms were sweaty, and the tag in the back of his T-shirt was scratchy. He thought he'd cut that out.

"I just wanted to protect you," she continued. "But I realized tonight that I've also been scared. And I've made too many decisions in my life based on fear, and I can't do that anymore."

Owen gritted his teeth. His subconscious was trying to tell him something. Trying to say, *See? You really knew all along. You just didn't want to believe it…* But he forced his mind to go blank. Forced his expression into an even, neutral look. Whatever she was going to tell him, he'd deal with it, and then they'd move on. How bad could it be?

"This baby is yours," she said softly. "Ours."

He blinked at her. And then there was a ringing in his ears.

Watching him, she leaned forward. Probably waiting for him to snap out of it. Have a heart attack or a stroke. Something.

"Owen?"

"What?" he croaked.

"It's yours."

He stared at her, and his body felt strange, numb. Like all the blood was pooling in his feet. The words that had just come out of her mouth made sense, but the concept didn't. *It's yours...* It wasn't something he could comprehend. At least, not while sitting there at the table like a department store mannequin.

Pushing slowly away from the table, he stood. The ringing in his ears was getting fainter. And his arms and legs were tingling. That must be the blood coming back. The problem was, his heart was now hammering so hard he could feel it in his bones. *It's yours...*

He looked down at Marley, and for the first time, he didn't like what he saw. Anger? Yeah. It hissed and sparked in his chest like a firecracker. And then it lit, becoming a bright, painful light behind his eyes. She'd let him believe this whole time... *This whole time.*

She must have recognized the look on his face, because she gazed up at him steadily. Knowingly.

"Say something," she whispered. "Please."

He rubbed circles on his chest. "Say something..." The fury simmered underneath his voice, making it crack. "I don't really know what to say, Marley."

"I don't blame you for how you're feeling."

"Well, that's big of you."

"I'm sorry, Owen. I didn't know how to tell you. Or even if I *should* tell you. With your career, it's so complicated. I thought I was doing the right thing."

His throat ached as he stared down at her. And for the first time, it occurred to him how it must have been for her. The shock of finding out. Being sick, exhausted. Shouldering it alone. But that wasn't enough to douse the anger behind his eyes. He wanted to feel it. He needed to feel it to sort out how he felt underneath.

"How could you let me think another guy was the father? All this time?"

"I thought I was protecting you."

"Protecting me? From what? The truth?"

She nodded miserably.

"I don't understand that. Were you ever going to tell me?"

"Of course. When you were picked up by a team. I didn't want you feeling like you had to stay because of this."

"Don't you think that should've been my choice?"

"Yes. You're absolutely right. But I wasn't coming from a rational place, Owen. I was scared." Her chin trembled, but she lifted it anyway. "My dad never wanted me. And then he left. I didn't think I could take that—I just didn't."

He clasped his hands on the back of his neck. "So, you thought I'd just *leave*? Is that what you think of me?"

"You told me that you didn't want to be a father. You said that."

His heartbeat slowed. He had said that. He remembered because it was true. He'd never wanted to be a father. Mostly because, deep down, he knew he'd fail miserably at it. That he'd probably end up being just like his old man, and he couldn't stomach the thought of doing that to a kid.

He took a deep breath and let it out slowly. "Why now?" he said. "Why tonight?"

"Because I saw how upset you were at AJ. And I realized that I was keeping this from you for the wrong reasons. And I couldn't go one more day without you knowing the truth. That's why."

There was a quiet strength in her expression. Like she absolutely expected him to turn away from this. It made him feel like shit. But maybe she knew him better than he knew himself, because he had no idea how he was going to handle it.

"I'm going to need some time with this, Marley,"

he said, crossing his arms over his chest. "I just need to process. I'll talk to you tomorrow, okay?"

She nodded. "Of course."

He thought about waking up and going for his morning run. About getting to the ballpark early for his workout and his usual talk with the coaches. About his routine that was always, always centered around baseball, around getting better and moving up. It was what he'd wanted for so long, he couldn't even remember when he hadn't wanted it. He didn't know how to identify as anything other than a ball player.

*A dad?* The thought terrified him. For so many reasons, it was impossible to count them all.

He watched as she slowly got up from the table, her thin cotton shirt clinging to her belly. She was several months along. He couldn't remember exactly how far. He had no idea what the baby would look like by now. There were books on this, of course, books that had pictures comparing the baby's size to an apple, to a grapefruit. Saying when it had fingernails and eyebrows. And all of a sudden, he felt like he might be sick.

She walked to the front door, and he followed her. He was still pissed. But other feelings were starting to seep in, too. Feelings that he couldn't identify yet. Who would've thought that ten minutes would've been enough to change his entire perspective on life? It was mind-numbing.

Opening the door, he looked down at his feet. "Good night, Marley. Drive safe."

"I will."

There was an emotional distance between them that he hated. He'd usually pull her into a hug at this point while fighting the near constant temptation to kiss her, imagining another night in bed with her and waking up with her in his arms. This chilliness was almost too much to take. But at the same time, he couldn't find it within himself to reach out to her. He was too confused. Too overwhelmed to do anything other than stand there and look at his stupid feet.

She walked past, and he caught the scent of her perfume. It stirred something inside his chest.

"Good night," she said. "See you tomorrow."

And he shut the door behind her, wondering what the hell just happened.

## *Chapter Ten*

Marley walked slowly up the gravel path of the old pioneer cemetery, the sun warm on her bare shoulders. At the top of the hill, there was a spot overlooking Cape Longing where a lovely red alder tree stood. Underneath that was her mother's simple marker. She hadn't been up here in years. And it was time.

Clutching the bouquet of daisies in her hand, she breathed in their perfumed scent mixed with the salty sea air. She looked back at Frances, who was leaning against the car. *I think you might need this time alone*, her foster mother had said. *I'll be right here when you get back...*

Marley lifted a hand and waved. Frances waved back. She'd been right. As much as Marley loved her foster mother, there was still a distinct ache for her birth mother. Or, at least, for some kind of memory of her, which she didn't have. The closest thing she'd ever had was this grave marker, some faded pictures and her baby book, where there were a few precious handwritten notes in the margins. But she'd always felt close to her here, and this was where she'd wanted to be today. Which also happened to be Marley's birthday.

She began walking again, trudging up the hillside that was alive with wind-weary coastal shrubs and golden Scotch broom. Below, she could hear the waves crashing against the cliffs and wondered what it must have been like in this cemetery one hundred and fifty years ago when Christmas Bay was just a tiny settlement. If she went all the way to the top of the hill, she knew she'd be able to see Frances's house, which had been there almost as long as the town itself.

After she'd been placed in foster care, sometimes Marley would come here with Stella and Kyla. They'd walk dreamily underneath the evergreens, making up romantic stories about Frances's house and the ghosts they were convinced lived there. Those were good memories during a time when there hadn't been many good things in Marley's life. Finding her foster family had saved her. And she knew if it came right down to it, they'd keep saving her. She wasn't alone. She had them.

And now she had this baby.

Swallowing down a sudden lump in her throat, she let her gaze settle on the small white stone peeking out of the long grass. The alder tree was just as it always had been, leaning over the grave with its protective branches stretched wide. Its leaves shivering in the coastal breeze. Marley remembered coming here the day her father had left, when she'd stood in the living room and hadn't known what to do. Hadn't known where to go, or who to call, or if she should wait, because he might come back. Just maybe. She'd run out the door and all the way up the hill when it became clear he wasn't coming back. Out of breath, her face streaked with dried tears, she had collapsed in the grass under the tree. Eventually, she'd stopped crying. Eventually, she'd been comforted by the cemetery's simple, quiet beauty. Exhaustion, fear and heartbreak had all demanded that she find comfort in something, so she had.

It was still beautiful all these years later. Still offering its comfort when she needed it most. It was a peaceful place for her mother.

She stepped up to the stone, bent to clear away the grass, then placed the daisies beside it.

Straightening slowly, she tucked her hair behind her ear.

"Hi, Mama," she said. "It's Marley."

The breeze blew through the tree's canopy as if in response. A squirrel chattered close by, and a redtailed hawk called in the distance. Then there was a certain quiet, a stillness that settled over the place where she stood that left her feeling peaceful.

"I know it's been a while since I've come to see you," she said. "But I think about you every day."

She felt her lips tremble with emotion, her heart thudding heavily against her breastbone. How could she miss someone she didn't even remember? She guessed it was the bond she missed. It was there even though her mom no longer was. The love was still there. She could feel it.

"A lot has happened since I was here last. I'm pregnant. I'm going to have a baby."

The breeze continued to blow, moving her hair against her face.

"I'm going to have a baby, and I think I'm in love. But I don't know how to be in love…"

She looked toward the horizon, where the ocean sparkled so brilliantly underneath the summer sun. It was beautiful and vast, and it took her breath away. She wondered right then what her mother would say to all of this. Would she judge, criticize? Or would she just listen and advise her daughter the best she could? Marley would never know.

Looking back at the sun-bleached marker, she licked her lips and continued with a tremor in her voice. "I wish you were here. But I try not to wish too hard, because it hurts too much. It's easier to accept things the way they are." She took a breath. "That's what I'm trying to do with this baby, with the father of this baby. But I'm going to need strength for that. I know you were strong. Living with Daddy probably made you that way. I hope I have some of that in me, too."

Tears had begun making their way down her cheeks, but she barely noticed.

"Anyway," she said quietly. "Don't worry about me. Frances is here. You would've liked her, Mama."

Gnats flitted around her face, and she waved them away. She stood there thinking about all those times she'd visited in the past. About all the times she'd visit in the future. It felt strange that this was the only relationship she'd ever have with her mom.

Kissing the tips of her fingers, she leaned down and touched them to the stone. "I'll be back soon, okay?"

The breeze blew the trees' branches back and forth, and it was like a gentle wave goodbye.

She turned and began making her way down the path again, the gravel crunching underneath her tennis shoes. Frances was waiting at the car, watching her with a hand shielding her eyes from the sun.

Her foster mother had forgotten they were coming today. Marley had had to remind her twice. She'd forgotten so much lately that it was hard not to be anxious about the future. But what she'd said just now was true. She was trying to accept things the way they were. From now on, she was going to make a conscious effort to be happy in the moment. She thought her mom would be proud of that. She knew Frances would be proud.

"Hey, birthday girl," Frances said as Marley got closer. "How about lunch and a pedicure?"

Marley smiled. She would always long for her mother. But she was so grateful for Frances, the only mother she'd ever known. And she loved her with all her heart.

"That sounds perfect," she said.

Owen shifted in his seat, trying to get comfortable. But it was no use. The bus was stuffy, they'd lost their game, and he had too much on his mind anyway.

He looked out the window at the darkened landscape illuminated by the full moon overhead. They'd be coming into Portland soon, where the lights glittered and the Willamette River flowed in midnight currents on the edge of the city.

Watching those lights in the distance, he knew how much opportunity awaited someone in a town like this. There was so much hustle, so much going on all the time. Unlike Christmas Bay, where the shops closed at sunset and the baseball was a hometown affair.

Still, as he leaned back against the headrest, he couldn't help but miss the little town he'd grown up in. And when had that happened exactly? Ever since he'd come back to play for the Sharks, it seemed like all he'd been able to think about was leaving again.

Mostly, that involved getting picked up by the majors. But sometimes he'd imagine washing out and leaving with nothing to show for his time there. Either way, he'd be leaving. That was what the plan had always been.

Now, as he stared out the smudged window and watched the sparkling city get closer, he recognized it wouldn't be that easy. If Marley decided to keep this baby, he would have a child there. And even if she didn't decide to keep it, *she* would be there.

Max shifted restlessly next to him, making the seat squeak. Owen looked over and smiled. His friend wore a sleep mask and a neck pillow, looking like he'd be more comfortable playing shuffleboard than minor-league baseball. Owen knew what he'd probably say about this whole thing with Marley, but he hadn't told him. In fact, he hadn't told anyone, choosing instead to chew on it every single second of every single hour until it felt like he might legitimately go nuts.

He looked back out the window. What he needed to do was talk to Marley. They hadn't spoken for a few days now, and the anger had finally subsided. In its place was a confusing mixture of emotion that scared the hell out of him. If he couldn't be mad at her anymore, who could he be mad at? The answer to that was pretty obvious. He was mad at himself.

He hadn't stopped himself that night of the party. He'd known very well how he felt about her, even then, and he'd chosen to break his own rules. Yes, they thought they'd been careful, but things happened anyway, like things usually did in life. And now there was a baby in the mix. And not only that, his heart was in the mix, too.

Looking at his watch, he blinked through blurry eyes. And then he saw the date. *The seventh.* He sat there for a minute, trying to remember if she'd said her birthday was on the seventh or the seventeenth. They'd talked about it last week. She'd said she was going to put some flowers on her mother's grave. Thinking he might offer to drive her, he'd checked the game schedule and saw that it fell on a day they had an away game...

He sighed. That was today. He'd been so preoccupied, he'd forgotten all about it. He could call her, but he didn't really want to do that on a crowded bus with everyone listening in. Max looked pretty dead to the world, but as soon as he heard anything remotely private being said, he'd probably sit up like Owen had put firecrackers in his seat.

He dug his phone out of his bag and held it for a minute, thinking. What was he supposed to say? *I can't get you out of my mind. I think I might love you. I have no idea how to be a father...*

It was that last part that made him grip the phone a little tighter. *Father.* The only example he'd ever known had left him a shell of a person for a very long time. And so what if he was unloved? That was okay, because he was popular, and that had filled in the gaps.

Owen was what he was. He'd come to accept certain things about himself. He was shallow because it was just easier that way. He buried his pain so it wouldn't be such an inconvenience. It was all well and good. It was the way he'd chosen to live his life up to this point. But the thought of dooming another human being to the same kind of dysfunction was simply a bridge too far.

He rubbed his thumb over the screen. He could tell her all these things. But doing that would open up old wounds that he'd spent a long time closing. Maybe someday. But not today.

Swiping the screen open, he typed a short message out. And then sent it.

Happy birthday. I've been thinking about you.

Marley took her headphones off and sat back in her chair with a sigh. On the field below, the maintenance crew was already starting to groom the dirt, and the crowd was filtering out the gates to the parking lot. It had been a good game. The Tiger Sharks had won after trailing three to one in the fourth inning. Owen had struck out Idaho's best hitter with a fastball that measured ninety-six miles per hour, not even his fastest on record. The crowd had gone wild, and his teammates had mobbed him in the dugout.

"Well, that was one for the books," Tony said, gathering up his things. He was wearing a Tiger Sharks baseball cap backward and a jersey with Owen's number on it.

And he wasn't the only one. She'd seen several number twenty-eights in the stands tonight. From little kids on their dads' shoulders to elderly ladies eating their popcorn. He was a bona fide celebrity, and Marley knew it wouldn't be long before the world was his oyster.

"It sure was," she said.

Tony nodded toward her stomach, which seemed to have popped out in the last few weeks. Frances and Kyla were convinced she was going to have a boy. She and Stella thought it was a girl. She was officially four months along and had gotten her first pair of maternity pants last week.

"How's the little one doing?" he asked.

She put a hand on her tummy. At the moment, she had gas, another lovely side effect of pregnancy. But he didn't need to know that. "Pretty good. I thought I felt the first kick the other day, but that might've been something I ate."

"Well, be prepared. Our oldest kept my wife up half the night with his kicking. Thought for sure he'd be a soccer player. He plays the piano now. Go figure."

"Right?"

He rubbed the back of his neck, looking like he wanted to say something. She watched him, waiting.

"It's none of my business," he finally said. "But I know you're doing this solo."

She swallowed hard. Christmas Bay was a small town and word got around. But the ballpark was even smaller, and it was no secret that Marley was single.

"I just wanted you to know that I'm here if you need anything," he continued awkwardly. "You know, like putting a crib together or moving furniture in. That kind of thing. It's hard having a kid. Lots of stuff to cross off the list before they get here."

Tony looked so anxious standing there—with his hands in his pockets and his gaze averted—that she wanted to give him a hug. She'd be fine on her own. But truthfully, she'd never thought of specifics like having to put a crib together. That might be a disaster of epic proportions.

"That's so sweet, Tony," she said. "You've all been so good to me. I'll definitely let you know. I might take you up on the furniture moving. I've got my eye on a rocking chair. I just have to pull the trigger."

He smiled. "Okay, good. Just holler when you decide."

"I will."

"Good night. See you tomorrow."

"See you tomorrow."

He walked out the door, leaving her alone in the announcer's box.

She looked down at the field again, where the stadium lights shone brightly on the maintenance crew.

Most of the players had probably gone home by now, but her gaze found its way to the locker rooms anyway. And her heart ached.

Biting her cheek, she forced herself to look away. She hadn't heard from him since the night of her birthday, when he'd sent that text. He said he'd been thinking about her. She'd sat there staring at it for at least five minutes, trying to decide how to answer. In the end, she'd sent a heart emoji back and had left it at that. If he wanted to talk to her, he would. Until then, she'd give him space. Space to let this settle. And time to figure out how he felt about it. God knew she'd needed the same thing.

Squaring her shoulders, she tucked her headphones in her desk drawer. She was trying her best not to think about much beyond that. Trying not to think about what she'd do if he didn't want anything to do with this baby. She expected him to leave—she kept telling herself she *wanted* him to. But of course, it was more complicated than that.

She stood and grabbed her purse, then walked out the door, locking it behind her. Her mind and her heart were all over the place. She just wanted to go home and crawl into bed. Tomorrow was Sunday, a day off, and it really couldn't come at a better time. She was exhausted.

Stepping down off the staircase, she dug her keys out of her purse.

"Hey."

She jumped at the sound of the voice beside her, then turned to see Owen standing there.

"Oh my *God*," she breathed. "You scared me to death."

He stepped toward her. He was freshly showered and wore jeans and a windbreaker tonight. Nothing jaw-dropping, but she had to work to keep her mouth closed anyway.

"Sorry," he said.

She hitched her purse up on her shoulder, trying to keep her composure. She hadn't been this close to him in days. Seeing him now, how blue his eyes were underneath the fluorescent lighting of the ballpark, how the stubble on his jaw was just a shade darker than his surfer blond hair, her heart squeezed painfully.

"Congratulations on the game," she said. "Ninety-six on the radar gun. You must be happy about that."

He shrugged. "I guess. Mostly I'm happy to see you."

The chilly ocean breeze brought his scent with it, and her stomach tightened. More than anything, she wanted to fall into those words and let them carry her away. But she didn't trust them not to crush her in the end.

"I'm happy to see you, too," she said quietly.

"How was your birthday?"

She'd spent the afternoon with Frances and had gone to dinner with her foster sisters. But it had also been a day full of emotion brought on by the visit to her mother's grave. And of course, the aftermath of telling Owen about the baby.

"It was nice," she said. Not wanting to get into the specifics. Definitely not wanting to cry again. She'd cried enough over the last few months to last a lifetime. Another pregnancy side effect.

"I'm sorry I didn't get to see you. With the game and everything…"

"You don't have to apologize. I know it was a lot to digest."

He watched her for a minute, and it was hard to tell what he was thinking. Across the park, the lights began switching off. It wouldn't be long before the stadium lights were off, too. The end of another day. One day closer to this baby being here. One day closer to having to make a decision. Marley squeezed her keys in her hands and felt them bite into her palm.

"I brought you something," he said.

"Oh yeah?"

"Pick a hand."

She tapped his left fist.

He opened it and held a small bag of peanuts out to her. "Your favorite."

She smiled. "You know the way to my heart."

"I try."

And then the stadium lights did switch off one by one, until the only light came from the parking lot next to them. The sky overhead was dark with clouds.

No stars or moon tonight, just steely gray clouds making their way across the heavens.

He cleared his throat. "Can I walk you to your car?"

"Sure. But it's just right over there."

"It's late, though. It'd make me feel better."

He opened the gate for her, and she walked through. Still clutching her keys. Still thinking about how fast this pregnancy was going and how unprepared she still felt deep down.

They walked slowly next to each other, their feet crunching on the gravel. Owen's shoulder brushed against hers, and his size and warmth made her feel safe. But she didn't want him to make her feel safe. She wanted to be okay on her own. She *had* to be okay on her own.

"How are you feeling?" he asked, his voice low.

"I'm fine. Tired from calling the game tonight, but fine."

"No, how are you feeling? Pregnancy-wise?"

"Oh." The breeze picked up and she pulled her sweater tight. "Good. No more bleeding. Everything is good."

He nodded, his hands buried in his jean pockets. His shoulders slumped, making him look younger than he actually was. He reminded her of a middle schooler getting ready to ask someone to a dance. Or break up with someone. She took a deep breath, realizing she hadn't taken one for a few seconds.

He came to a stop and touched her elbow.

She turned to look up at him with a nervous feeling in her stomach.

"I've been thinking a lot since the other night," he said. "Since you told me about the baby."

The nervous feeling became more of an acute pain. No matter what happened in Marley's life, no matter how many good things accumulated for her, she realized right then that she'd probably always anticipate the bad. Expect it in a way that normal people wouldn't. Her dad's leaving had made her weird. And the realization made her furious all over again. At him, at herself.

She forced her chin up and waited for what she knew was coming. She could see it on his face. She could read it in his eyes. He wasn't ready for this. Maybe he'd never be ready, and that was okay. Because she was ready. It wasn't until right then, until that very moment, that she knew she was going to keep this baby. It would be wanted. At least by one of its parents. She wouldn't, she *couldn't*, walk away from it.

"The thought of being a dad," he said, his voice hoarse. "It scares me so much, it's not really something that I can articulate."

She watched him. Saw the raw emotion pass over his features. But she kept quiet because she was scared, too.

"I've gone over and over it," he continued. "Thought about what to do, how to help you, how to be a decent man. And I know most people would say that would be to stay and raise their kid. And they'd be right. In most cases, they'd be absolutely right. But my dad stayed, and he affected me in ways that I'm still trying to unpack, to be honest."

She nodded, feeling mildly sick. She understood this line of thinking. But leaving cut, too. Her dad had left, and she was just as screwed up by it. She wondered if there would ever be a right choice for him.

"There's no doubt in my mind that I'm falling in love with you," he said softly.

She stared up at him.

"And I've been trying to figure out what to do about that. Do I stay and try to make it work? Or do I leave and support you and the baby the best way I know how? By playing ball. By making money for you both. By not breaking your heart…"

She swallowed with some difficulty, but her throat still ached. Her eyes still stung. She pulled her sweater tighter around her shoulders, but she still felt cold. None of the pregnancy books prepared you for this kind of scenario. What to do if the father of your baby decided he loved you but just couldn't be a father. After this, she'd probably be able to write the chapter herself.

"I started falling for you a long time ago," she said.

He smiled, and two long dimples cut into each scruffy cheek. For a minute, she could almost imagine it working out between them. They were falling in love. They were going to have a baby. In a movie, that was all you'd need. But this wasn't a movie. It was real life, and they had real issues that couldn't be fixed with a simple declaration of love underneath a night sky. It was going to take more than that. And she just wasn't sure it was in the cards for them.

"You're a good man, Owen," she continued. "I know you're going to struggle with this, and that's okay. But I want you to know I'm not going to hold it against you for leaving. That's what I want for you. Your career. Your dream."

He shook his head. "I don't know..."

"It took me a while to decide what I wanted to do," she said. "I thought about adoption, but I know I won't be able to give this baby up. That's what's right for me. What's right for me doesn't have to be right for you. It doesn't mean you won't be supportive, and it doesn't mean we can't still love each other. There are all kinds of families. We don't have to be together to care about each other."

He was quiet at that.

She reached out and took his hand. It was warm, rough with calluses. And she thought about how these very hands had moved over her body four months ago. If she'd known then what she knew now, would she have changed anything? She didn't think she would. As messed up as it felt sometimes, this was exactly where she needed to be. She'd learn from this.

She'd grow from it. And at the end of the day, she'd have a little baby that she would love dearly.

"I'm going to be honest with you," she continued. "And it's not easy to say this…"

He waited, watching her.

"But I need to distance myself from you, Owen. Just enough so that when you leave, I won't be so sad. And I'll be able to concentrate on this baby and all the things that will go along with it. I'm going to need my head in a good place for this."

He dug his hands farther into his pockets. His windbreaker stretched over his broad shoulders, and he looked so good that it actually hurt. She schooled her features, willing herself to breathe easy. Not to think about what this actually meant. Saying good-bye.

"I understand," he said. "Staying away from you will be hard. But leaving will be harder."

She nodded, not trusting herself to speak.

"I'm going to be back, though," he continued quietly. "I'll send money, of course. I'll see you and the baby. Unless you don't want me to…"

"Of course I'll want you to. We'll figure it out. We have time. But for now, I think this is what's best for us. For all of us, right?"

His gaze settled on hers. It would be easier if she didn't believe what he'd said about falling in love with her. But at that moment, she did believe it. It was written all over his face.

Her throat tightened, and all of a sudden, she was desperate to get away. To leave here without crying, without him pulling her into a hug. If she and Owen were going to step away from each other, they needed to do it now. Before they got too deep to dig themselves out.

She jingled her keys in her hand. "I'd better get going," she said. "I have a few stops to make before I go home, so…"

He stepped back. "Sure."

With one more look at him, she opened her car door and climbed inside.

And managed to drive away before starting to sob.

## Chapter Eleven

*Father...baby...Marley...*

Owen shut his eyes, trying to clear his head. He'd been trying to clear it for days now, but nothing was working. Not baseball, not hanging out with the guys after the games, not even fishing, which usually did the trick when his life really turned to garbage. The thoughts kept creeping in. Along with the feelings. Along with the heartbreak.

He squeezed the ball in his hand, pushing it into the soft leather of his glove. *Marley...* The cool ocean breeze blew against his skin, cooling it. It smelled salty, like fish. Like home. *Baby...* He kept his eyes shut, trying to focus. Trying to push everything else away.

And then he opened his eyes, lifted his leg, shifted

his weight and let the ball fly. It sailed past the padded target and bounced with a clang against the chain-link fence.

Frowning, he pulled his hat low over his eyes.

His pitching coach frowned, too. And eyed him with his hands on his hips.

"What the hell, Taylor?"

"I know," he said. "Just having an off day."

"You're having an off *week*. I want you to focus this time. Really load that hip during your forward move. You want the force to stabilize your drive leg." He patted his own thigh for emphasis. "You've got enough muscle and size for it. Do it again."

Owen nodded as his coach threw the ball back, and he caught it with a sharp *thwack* in his glove. *Marley... baby...* His heart beat heavily inside his chest. It ached. It had been aching for days. Every time he saw her pulling up to the ballpark, every time he saw her walking down the steps from the announcer's box, every time he heard her voice through the loudspeakers, it felt like his body was trying to turn itself inside out. He hadn't been able to eat; he hadn't been able to sleep. The talk they'd had last week hadn't been the end of something. It had been the beginning of it. A misery that he hadn't known existed until now.

Closing his eyes again, he took a deep breath and, this time, managed to clear his head of everything. A numbness settled over him, and he squeezed the ball in his hand. Again, he lifted his leg, drew his arm back and fired.

The ball flew through the air like a bullet. Nothing but a white streak that hit the padded target with a reverberating smack.

His pitching coach grinned. "That's more like it. You need to be asking yourself about that back foot posture. Much better this time. And where's your trunk and your rear shoulder? You want a good stretch when you launch. Nice job."

Owen nodded as his coach threw the ball back. He caught it in his glove and wiped some sweat off his brow. He wished the breeze would pick up again. In fact, he wished a storm would blow in and they'd cancel tomorrow's game. He just wanted to sit and think. Think for days, if that was what it took to find some peace with this. With the decision he'd made so quickly in the parking lot the other night.

How had this happened? They'd confessed to falling for each other but had somehow ended up apart.

He knew how. It wasn't just love they were talking about, and it wasn't just each other. There was a baby to consider, and that little baby was the most important thing of all. As it absolutely should be. But what bothered Owen the most was the question he kept asking himself over and over again. What kind of man just walked away from his child like this? No matter how chicken he was. No matter how worried he was he would screw it up.

He loved baseball. But was it his entire life? He

kept thinking about what Max said that day in the gym—that there was more to life than baseball. Was Marley his more than baseball? Was this baby? He didn't know yet, but he needed time to figure it out.

"Let's go, Taylor," his coach said, taking his baseball cap off and running a hand through his balding hair. "You're slower than molasses, son."

Smiling, Owen rubbed the ball into his glove, starting to feel calm for the first time in a week. He just needed more time, that was all. Maybe they could make this work. Somehow, some way, maybe they didn't have to say goodbye yet.

And it was Marley's name that kept dancing through his head as he wound up for another pitch.

"How about this one?"

Marley turned away from the window at Coastal Sweets to see that Stella had another baby furniture catalog open. She had her finger on a picture of a dark cherrywood crib.

Stepping over to the counter, Marley looked down at it. It was beautiful. But it wasn't the right one. She kept thinking she'd know it when she saw it, but this was the third catalog they'd been through this morning, and she was starting to think something else was going on here. Maybe she just didn't want to be picking out a crib while she still felt so sad.

She shook her head. "I was thinking of a lighter wood. Something bright and cheerful."

"Do you know what color the nursery is going to be?"

"Periwinkle," she said emphatically. "It reminds me of the ocean."

"Oh, I love periwinkle." Stella reached over and scratched Beauregard behind the ears. He was lounging in his princess bed next to the cash register, looking fat as a tick. "You're going to need a rocker, too," she said. "Do you have one in mind?"

Marley leaned against the counter and put her hand on her belly. "Actually, I do. It's at the antique shop down the street. And Tony even said he'd pick it up for me."

"Why Tony? Doesn't Owen have a truck?"

"He does…"

Her foster sister watched her closely.

"But I told him it would be better if we don't see each other right now," she said.

"Marley…"

"I know. I know what you're going to say. He might get used to the idea, and maybe he'd want to stay. But that's the thing. I don't want him to stay, not like this. He'd only end up resenting it."

"I just hate to see you give up this fast."

"I'm not giving up," she said. "I'm letting go of potential heartbreak. By cutting it off now, there's less chance of getting tangled up in something we can't get untangled from."

"Well…I'd say you're already pretty tangled."

Marley gave her a small smile. "Yeah. We are. But

right now, we really care for each other. Why ruin that? He's not dad material. He said so himself. You know what my dad did. That's what happens when you force it."

*When you force it...* She'd used Owen's own words there, and Stella frowned. If there was one thing her sister understood, that they all understood, it was family abandonment.

"I just want you to be happy," Stella said. "That's all."

Marley wasn't so sure about happy. But happiness was relative, anyway.

She took an even breath. The shop smelled comforting and familiar. Like spun sugar and the beach. It brought her right back to middle school, when she'd first come to live with Frances. All three girls had spent their summers working at Coastal Sweets, which looked like something out of a Hallmark movie. The building itself was over one hundred years old and was an absolute charmer with its black-and-white awnings that stretched over the sidewalks, where colorful flower baskets hung in the spring and summer.

She took the lid off the jar on the counter and picked out a Tootsie Pop—cherry, her favorite. She unwrapped it and put it in her mouth, savoring the tangy sweetness.

Taking it out again, she licked her lips. "How's Frances, Stella? How are things in the shop?"

Their foster mother had taken the day off. She had a hair appointment that afternoon, and Stella had convinced her to sleep in. But normally she'd be there front and center, stocking the shelves, cleaning the windows and bins, sweeping the floor. She adored the shop. Even with her Alzheimer's diagnosis, she planned on being a presence there as long as she could. It was what made her the happiest.

Stella gave Beauregard one more pat. He was purring now, loud and hoarse. "She's doing okay," she said. "But I had to take the books over. I think we're going to have to hire someone for that pretty soon. To take some of the load off."

Marley nodded. At the moment, Kyla was helping in the shop, too, but she'd go back to school in the fall, and then it would just be Stella and Frances again. They really needed to hire someone else or scale back hours, but Frances wasn't ready to do that yet. She could be stubborn as a mule when it came to what she wanted. And right now, she wanted things to stay the same, even though they were changing fast. A simple fact that made Marley's heart ache.

But if there was any kind of silver lining to Frances's memory loss, it was that it had brought them all back together again. It had brought them home.

She looked out the window at the people walking by. They held shopping bags and ice cream cones, stopping every now and then to peer in the window. She still had a hard time believing she was back in Christmas Bay. But now that she was here, she couldn't imagine being anywhere else. It was as if the bad memories were slowly being taken over by the good ones. By all those years living in Frances's lovely old house.

Of summers working at Coastal Sweets. Of balmy evenings at the baseball field. And now of Owen, too.

She rested her hand on her stomach. No matter what happened in the months to come, she'd always hold those things close to her heart. Like Stella had said, she and Owen were tangled up in each other. They always would be. And even though they might not end up with a fairy-tale ending, it could be happy enough with the passage of time. They'd each write their own happy ending.

"What's going on in that head of yours?" Stella asked. "I can see the wheels turning."

Marley smiled over her shoulder. "Just thinking. Life is weird, isn't it?"

"Life is really weird. But it can be really good."

Marley nodded, looking out the window again. The sun had been hiding behind puffy white clouds all morning but had finally come out, shining through the window and warming up the shop with its long fingers of gold.

From now on, she was just going to focus on the good. There was enough of it to go around.

Owen turned his baseball cap around and stepped back to look at the slash of paint on the wall.

"What do you think?" he asked. Then he turned to Max, who was standing behind him with a confused look on his face.

"It's pink."

"It's not pink. It's beige."

"It looks pink to me."

"The sales guy said it was warm beige. That's what he said. It's supposed to be gender neutral."

Max took a sip of his beer. "Says who?"

"Says the sales guy."

"I think you need a second opinion."

"That's what you're for."

"I mean from someone who knows what they're talking about. There's a reason all my walls are white, man."

Owen sighed. This was turning out to be harder than he'd thought. The painting of his spare room was supposed to be the easy part. The therapeutic part. The first step where he really started exploring the idea of being a part of this baby's life.

Staring at the wall, he gritted his teeth. If he was getting stumped right out of the gate on something like this, he couldn't hold out much hope for the rest of it.

"What about green?" Max said, narrowing his eyes at the paint streak. "Or yellow? Aren't those supposed to be gender neutral?"

"Hell, I don't know. Do you think I should get some green?"

"I don't think the kid is going to know the difference," Max said evenly. "If you'd told me about this *sooner*, I might have some better ideas for you. I might've had some time to think about it and work my magic. But, you know. You just mentioned it the other damn day." He took another slurp of his beer, clearly sulking now.

Owen smiled and slapped him on the back. "I know, buddy. But I haven't told anyone. Only you. Does that make you feel better?"

"A little," Max mumbled.

"And I promise I'll keep you in the loop from now on."

"I mean, I'd appreciate that."

"And I'm sorry I didn't tell you sooner."

"I forgive you."

"All good now?"

Max sniffed and paused dramatically. "It's all good," he finally said. "And you should be reading *What to Expect When You're Expecting*. Just FYI."

"Okay…"

"Yeah, my sister got it when she found out she was going to have a baby, and it's like pregnancy for dummies. Not that first-time moms are dummies or anything, but they don't know what they don't know. And there's a section for dads, too. She made my brother-in-law read it and take notes."

"Wow," Owen said. "You really know your pregnancy literature."

Max shrugged. "That's what I'm saying. You need to tell me these things. I can help you out."

"I'm not planning on this happening again."

"Well, you didn't plan on it happening this time, either…"

Owen couldn't argue with that. Instead, he rubbed

his chin and looked back at the wall. The last few weeks away from Marley had been the most unhappy of his life. And that was saying something, because he'd had some fairly shitty times. He missed her. He missed talking to her, touching her, laughing with her. He missed everything about her.

And then he'd started thinking about how it would be to try to parent from another city. He had no idea if he could actually do this and do it right. There would be so many opportunities to screw it up. But there would also be opportunities to get it right, and the thought of those were what made him go out and buy paint. And tell Max.

He kept thinking about what one of his buddies had said about being a father—*If you do it at least 50 percent right, you're doing a pretty good job.*

Maybe he could handle 50 percent.

Marley looked down at the text on her phone and frowned, annoyed that her heart jumped at the words. She was just starting to settle into her life without Owen. She was just beginning to see herself doing this without him, and now this.

Frances watched from across the kitchen table. It was a stormy Saturday afternoon, and the game that evening had been canceled, so they were getting to spend the day together. A rare and unexpected treat.

When Marley had walked through the door of the old Victorian, it had been like a balm for her soul. The warm yellow light spilling from the antique lamps in the corners. A crackling fire in the redbrick hearth. Beauregard curled in a purring black-and-white ball on the sofa.

Outside, the ocean churned grumpy and gray at the base of the cliffs, and the rain was coming in sheets. But inside, it was like stepping into soft, cozy slippers. Frances even had hot chocolate and cinnamon toast waiting for her on the table, her favorite childhood snack.

She sat there now, feeling some of that warmth ease away.

"What is it?" Frances asked, setting her mug down.

She looked up. "Owen. He just texted me."

"And?"

"He said he misses me."

A gust of wind blew against the single-paned windows, rattling them. Beauregard looked up from his spot on the couch, then stretched dramatically, totally unconcerned with the weather.

"Do you miss him?" Frances asked.

Marley sighed and wrapped her hands around her steaming mug. "I do."

"Then why don't you tell him?"

It seemed so simple. And she guessed for a lot of people, it might be. But for her, there would always be an almost paralyzing fear that came with letting herself get too close. With letting herself trust.

"Because opening that door isn't smart," she said. "I need this time to get over him."

"But maybe if you text him back, you'll see that keeping in touch won't be as hard as you think."

The undeniable fluttering of her heart said otherwise. But she smiled at her foster mother to reassure her. And maybe to reassure herself, too. "I won't leave him hanging. I just need to figure out what to say so I don't encourage this. So I don't go falling in love again."

Frances watched her with a knowing look on her face. "Again?"

Marley took a sip of her hot chocolate and burned her tongue. Wincing, she set it down again. "Okay. I haven't really stopped loving him…"

"I know you're trying to control this, honey, but love has a way of doing what it wants."

She frowned, looking down at her hands.

"I can't tell you I understand exactly how you feel," Frances continued, "because I've never been in your shoes. But I *can* tell you that I understand what it feels like to be young and in love. Maybe you can just trust where it's leading you."

She looked up at her foster mother and shook her head. "I can't do that, Frances. I can't let myself need him and then have him walk away."

"Do you think he would?"

"I think he's going to leave for baseball. And he

*should* leave for baseball. That's what I want for him."

Frances's expression fell. "Sweetheart. Is that what you really want?"

Marley had spent a lot of time telling herself that it was. But deep down, she wasn't so sure. The whole truth was, she wanted him to stay. But she also wanted to be *enough* for him to stay. Without baseball in the mix. Without even the baby in the mix, and she didn't like how selfish that felt.

"I want him to be happy," she said quietly. "I guess that's what I want."

"And you want to be happy, too."

She nodded. *That, too.*

## *Chapter Twelve*

Owen made his way through the furniture store with a frown. He'd driven into Eugene because there were more choices here than in Christmas Bay, but now he wished he'd just stayed home and gone to that vintage place on Main Street. They'd probably have cribs. Old ones, but still. A hell of a lot nicer than this box-store stuff.

He ran a hand through his hair and felt that familiar tightening of his stomach at the thought of having an actual nursery in his house. After the painting a few weeks ago, he'd gone into some weird robotic mode, working on the room after games and on his days off, not really letting himself think too much, until one afternoon, he'd stepped back and it was finished. The only thing left was the crib.

He stopped in front of a changing table now and ran his fingers along the glossy wood finish. He imagined a baby lying there, needing to be changed. Kicking its feet and waving its fists in the air. He was going to be a dad. Sometime between the beige paint that Max insisted was pink and wondering if a car seat would fit in his truck, he'd realized that it didn't matter if he was ready for this or not. It didn't matter if he was committed or not. It was happening anyway.

He sighed, thinking of the text he'd sent Marley the other day. He'd sent it the exact moment that the weird, robotic feeling had given way to a tidal wave of emotion that had nearly knocked him off his feet. He knew she needed space; he knew she needed time. He understood all that, but he'd simply missed her. And wanted her to know.

But it had blown up in his face, because she'd been pretty clear the second time around. She wanted distance. So he hadn't told her about the nursery. He hadn't told her anything, and that numb feeling had come right back again. Protecting him. Allowing him to move through his days in a safe, detached way. Yes, the baby was coming. But he could still do the easiest thing and support them from afar. It was definitely chickenshit. But it was a damn sight better than his own father had done, and that gave him some measure of comfort. Not a lot, but a little.

His phone rang from his back pocket, and he dug it out to see his coach's name on the screen.

"Hello?"

"Hey, Taylor."

"Coach. What's up?"

"Pack your bags. Dan Martel just called. They want you in Seattle for a workout next weekend."

Owen's heart thumped in his neck. "Dan Martel?"

"The scouting director."

All of a sudden, his legs felt weak, and he leaned against the changing table. This was it. This was the moment he'd been waiting for. If he could manage to impress them at this workout, the chances of them picking him up were very good. And the fact that Dan Martel had called himself? Even better.

But then he thought of Marley, and his heartbeat slowed. He thought of the baby. The little baby whose crib he was shopping for that very moment.

"Taylor?"

"Yeah, I'm here."

"What's wrong? This is good news, son."

"I know. I know it's good."

"Then what?"

"Nothing. Just…life stuff."

"Well, you'd better focus. Because unless someone's dead or dying, life stuff does not take precedence over a workout in Seattle, got it?"

"Got it."

His coach was a good guy. A family man. He wondered what he'd say if Owen were completely honest right then. If he told him he had a baby on the way. Maybe he'd understand and maybe he wouldn't. Like Marley, he also wanted the majors for Owen. He was proud of him and had made it clear at the beginning of the season that before retiring next year, his goal was to see his star pitcher sign a big-league contract. Family man or not, Owen doubted he'd be in the right frame of mind after that phone call from Washington to hear any excuses. Especially if someone wasn't dead or dying.

He gritted his teeth, feeling the muscles in his jaw bunch almost painfully. No, this wasn't the time to voice any kind of hesitation, any kind of doubt. His job was to get in the zone and stay there. And if he got on with the Mariners, this was what fatherhood would look like, anyway. At least during the season, when he'd have to do it from another state.

"Taylor?"

His coach's voice sounded about a thousand miles away. *Another state.* This was what he'd dreamed about since he was a kid, standing on the pitcher's mound at Christmas Bay High School with his father's cruel words reverberating in his ears. *You're never gonna amount to anything...* He'd always told himself he'd prove him wrong. And this was his chance. Leaving was what he'd always wanted. So, why did it feel so wrong?

"I'm here," he said, his voice low.

"So, you'll need to catch the red-eye after the game next Thursday. Are you ready for this? Really ready?"

He was. And he wasn't.

"I'm ready," he said, hoping he sounded convincing. "Bring it on."

Marley stood in front of her open closet, staring at her clothes. None of them really fit anymore. At least, not the ones for the bottom half of her body. She could still do T-shirts, flannels, her trademark blouses at work. But she was going to have to go shopping for more than maternity pants soon. At the rate she was going, in another month or two, she was going to look like she'd swallowed a basketball, and by then, even the flannels wouldn't fit anymore.

She lifted up her shirt now and rubbed her bare belly. And then felt the faintest fluttery kick. She grinned. At first it had been hard to tell the difference between the kicks and the gas bubbles, but now she could definitely tell. So far, though, it had never happened when she'd been in the room with anyone else. If it had, she would've grabbed their hand and pressed it to her stomach. She wanted to share this. But what she really wanted was to share it with Owen.

At the thought of him, she looked back at her clothes, trying to ignore the hopeful ache in her heart. Despite lecturing herself about keeping her distance, she hadn't been able to stop thinking about that text he'd sent. *I miss you...*

She'd ended up telling him that she missed him, too, but she still wasn't ready to see him yet. But the truth was, she couldn't wait to see him. Tomorrow was a home game, and that was why she was standing in front of her closet now, surveying her clothes for something flattering to wear. Something that would accentuate the soft swell of her stomach, which she'd come to love. Something that would set off the color of her eyes and the glow of her skin. She'd been told she was glowing lately. If that were true, she was going to have to play it up for as long as possible, as she didn't think she'd ever glowed before in her life.

There was a knock at the front door, and she startled. She wasn't expecting anyone, but Kyla had made a habit of stopping by with ice cream lately, so maybe it was her.

After a quick look in the mirror, Marley padded to the door in her bare feet and opened it with a smile.

But it wasn't Kyla standing there on the stoop. It was Owen.

Blood rushed to her cheeks as she stared up at him, too surprised to speak. He looked gorgeous today. Tan and muscular in a dark gray T-shirt and faded jeans. Eyes so blue they made her knees weak.

"Owen," she said, touching her ponytail self-consciously. "What are you doing here?"

"Sorry. I know we're supposed to be doing the whole space thing, but I needed to see you. Is this a bad time?"

"No. I look awful, though. It's a chore day."

He looked down at her in that way he had. That way that made her feel beautiful, desirable, even when she hadn't showered yet. Nobody had ever made her feel as pretty as Owen did. Nobody.

"You look stunning," he said softly. "But you always do."

She smiled. "You're a charmer, number twenty-eight."

"Can I come in? I promise I won't stay long."

"Of course." There was an urgency to his voice that sent a prickle of unease up her spine. "Do you want some coffee? Tea? Antacid? I've been drinking that like it's going out of style."

He frowned as she shut the door. "Are you feeling okay?"

"Indigestion. You get used to it."

He watched her for a long moment, and her heart skipped in anticipation. He had that effect.

She clasped her hands in front of her belly, hoping she didn't look as flustered as she felt. Hoping she looked grounded and cool and not in love. "So," she said evenly, "what gives?"

"I just have some news. Some good news, and I wanted you to hear it from me first."

"What is it?"

"Coach called today," he said. "I guess Dan Martel wants me to come for a workout."

She stared at him. "Dan Martel? *The* Dan Martel?"

"The one and only."

She clapped her hands in excitement. "Oh my God, Owen. That's fantastic! I'm so, so proud of you!"

He shrugged, rocking back on his feet. "Well, you know. This doesn't mean anything yet."

"No, but it's a really good sign." She grinned, so happy for him, she thought she might crack wide open. But at the same time, she thought her heart might crack open, too. Because this was it. Truly. The beginning of something very different. They would be going their separate ways now and settling into a new normal. Whatever that looked like.

"When are you going?" she asked.

"Next Thursday. After the game."

"Oh, wow," she said. "That's…that's really fast. You must be so excited, Owen." She was trying hard to school her features. Trying to hold on to that spark of happiness. For both of them.

But the reality was, when he'd sent that text, she'd allowed herself to hope. Just a little, but it was a sliver that had buried itself inside of her, and she'd allowed it to grow. She was so mad at herself for that. He wasn't going to stay here, and she'd never ask him to. He was a rocket about to be launched to the moon.

Putting his hands in his pockets, he gazed down at her. She breathed in his scent, so warm and sexy, so uniquely him that it always made her want to throw her arms around him and bury her face in his chest. She really was a mess.

"You are one beautiful woman, Marley Carmichael," he said, his voice husky. "Do you know that?"

She had to consciously lock her knees in place. If he kept this up, she wouldn't be able to take two steps away from him, much less the thousand miles they'd need to start their new lives.

He didn't wait for her to answer. "Why do I have a feeling you *don't* know that?"

"Well, look at me."

"I am looking at you."

She could feel the crack in her heart begin to grow. How long before it would break in half?

"Owen…" she began.

He reached out and cupped her cheek, surprising her. His skin was rough, but his touch was soft as satin. He was a walking contradiction.

"I've been thinking about things," he said.

She waited, her pulse tapping behind her ears. *Please don't do this*, she thought. *Don't make me fall any harder than I already have. Don't break my heart any more than it already is.*

"And what I said the other day is true," he continued. "I miss you, Marley."

She shook her head, then reached up and gently moved his hand away. "I can't do this," she said. "I can't."

"It doesn't have to be that hard."

Now he sounded like Frances. It didn't have to be hard, but it *was* hard. That was the reality. And they both needed to face it.

She lifted her chin, wanting to say something to make him go. Because if he didn't leave soon, she wasn't going to have the strength to fight this. And right then, it felt like her very survival depended on it.

"You don't want kids," she said evenly.

"I know what I said."

"You're still a kid yourself. Your house is a mess, you flirt with everyone..."

His mouth settled into a thin line. "That's not true."

She raised her eyebrows.

"Okay," he said. "Maybe before, but not now."

"Women throw themselves at you. Everywhere you go. I've seen it. You can't really expect me to believe you've changed that much."

His jaw muscles bunched, his expression cool.

If she wanted him to leave, if she wanted him to walk out that door and spare her heart any more of this trauma, she knew she needed to end it. Now.

"You wouldn't be any good at this, Owen."

He narrowed his eyes at her. This was the same conversation they'd had the night they'd slept together. They'd both acknowledged they didn't want anything more and why. His words that night hadn't been much different than her words just now, but somehow what she'd said now *had* been different. Because she could clearly see that she'd hurt him.

She'd wanted him to leave. She hadn't wanted to be cruel, and she immediately wished she could take it back.

She reached out, and he stepped back.

"No," he said, his voice dangerously low. "Don't."

"I didn't mean—"

"I know what you meant."

"You're a great guy. You're just not ready for this."

"Do me a favor, Marley, and stop telling me what I'm not ready for."

Her heart sank. "I'm just trying to be realistic. And I'm trying to protect us both."

"From me."

"That's not what I said."

"But it's what you meant."

She bit her cheek. Hard. It was what she'd meant, but not necessarily in that way. She was scared of being hurt, of being abandoned, and no matter how it sounded coming out of her mouth, it was true that he was the one who wielded that power here.

But it was pretty obvious he was in no state of mind to hear that right now. And she was in no state of mind to be able to explain it without fumbling and making it worse.

"I can see by your silence," he said, "that I'm right."

Tears filled her eyes. If she hadn't been sure she loved him before, she was absolutely certain now. Because hurting him felt like hurting herself. It felt like a knife to her own heart. Cold, sharp steel slicing through warm flesh.

"It's okay," he said evenly. He took another step back toward the door. And took his warmth, his vitality, with him. "My old man didn't think I'd measure up, either."

She shook her head miserably. "That's not it…"

"I just thought you'd see me differently than everyone else. I thought you'd give me a chance."

"But when we talked," she said. "At the ballpark. You told me you didn't want this. You told me you were scared."

"I *am* scared, Marley. I'm scared to death. But I came here to—" He stopped short. "You know what? It doesn't matter what I came here for. You're right, and I don't blame you for how you feel. I blame myself."

"Why?" The tears were dripping from her chin now, onto her collarbone. She didn't bother wiping them away. She just wanted the floor to open up and swallow her whole.

"For thinking I could do this." He laughed bitterly. "What a joke."

"Owen."

He stepped toward her then, and all of a sudden, he was so close that she could see the individual spikes of stubble on his chin. He was breathing heavily, and his eyes were sharp. He reached out and took her face in his hands, cradling it with his trademark gentleness, even though she could feel the pent-up energy in his touch.

He tilted her head back until she was looking directly into his eyes. Until the tears were sliding down her throat in a salty trail.

And then he kissed her. With all the passion and urgency from the night their baby was conceived. He slid his hand into her hair and cupped the back of her head. He urged her lips open with his tongue, and she invited him inside, trembling now and pushing herself into him. Unable to get close enough.

She heard herself whimper and realized she was clinging to him. Digging her fingers into his shoulders. Saying with her body what she couldn't bring herself to say out loud. *Stay with me, don't leave us...*

And then, just as quickly as he'd leaned in to kiss her, he broke it again. Then stepped back.

She tried to steady herself. Tried to regain her equilibrium, but it was no use. She felt like she was moving underwater, struggling to break the surface for a full breath.

"Call me crazy," he said, his voice gravelly, "but that did not seem like a woman who wants to say goodbye."

She licked her lips. "That's the problem, Owen. Saying goodbye to you is going to break my heart. Don't you see that?"

"I get it, believe me. My heart is already toast, and now I'm leaving, and I might be leaving for good, and I feel like hell. All the way around. I won't have you. I won't have the baby. But I'll sure as hell have baseball. Always baseball."

It was the first time she'd ever heard him talk like this. It wasn't like him. It unsettled her, maybe more than his kiss had.

"It's what you've always wanted," she said. "You should be happy."

"Right now, nothing is going to make me happy."

Did he mean staying? Or going? She guessed he meant both. It didn't matter anyway. She didn't trust herself to answer him. Because if she said anything at all, if she opened her mouth, it would be to ask him to hold her. To kiss her again. And not to leave.

So she stayed quiet, wanting to believe she was doing it for him. But knowing deep down in the darkest, loneliest parts of her heart that she was doing it because of that old fear born of her father leaving. That abandonment had punched an ugly hole inside of her that she'd spent a lifetime trying to fill.

Owen rubbed the stubble on his chin, looking restless and wild. It was possible that after this, after leaving today, he might not want anything to do with her or the baby. That was all she kept thinking. *What if, what if, what if...* He'd said he wanted a chance. But he couldn't possibly understand how big of an ask that was. It was basically asking her to jump blind. But it wasn't only she who'd be jumping— she'd be taking the baby with her, too.

An expression settled on his face then that she couldn't read. It was like a wall was going up. Something to keep her out. Or keep himself in. She understood it, though, because she had those same walls.

"I'm going to go," he said, his voice low. "I told Coach I'd come in early and get the details for Thursday."

She nodded, numb. This wouldn't sting so much

if he'd turned out to be the jerk she'd always thought he was. If he'd turned out like his father or her father or Kyla's or Stella's. He might not be ready for a baby, but she knew he wasn't like any of them. He was a good and decent man who was simply struggling with this. Just like she was.

She wondered why that common bond wasn't enough right then. It should've been. But life was complicated. And it didn't always give you what you wished for. She knew that better than most. She'd spent her entire childhood wishing for things that had little to no chance of materializing.

So she watched him turn his back and reach for the door. It was what she'd been dreading this whole time, and it hurt just as much as she'd thought it would.

"Owen," she said softly.

He turned to her again, and she still couldn't read him. He was as far away as he'd ever been.

"No matter what," she continued, "I love you."

He watched her for another few seconds.

And then he was gone. Like she always knew he would be.

## Chapter Thirteen

Marley sat on the examination table with the familiar pink gown wrapped snug around her legs. Her heart thumped steadily, a rhythm she could feel throughout her entire body.

She breathed in the sterile scent of the room and looked over at Frances, who was thumbing through a *People* magazine with her thick black-framed readers sliding down her nose.

Her foster mother glanced up and frowned. "Honey, tell me what this appointment is for again?"

The words sent a sharp pang through Marley's chest. She'd just reminded her a few minutes ago. This was the five-month ultrasound. The appointment where they were going to find out the sex of the baby. They'd been looking forward to it for weeks.

But Frances couldn't seem to hold on to any of that information. As soon as it was given to her, it slipped right out of her grasp again, floating away like a child's balloon into a clear blue sky.

Marley forced a lighthearted smile. "It's the appointment where we find out whether it's a boy or a girl."

"*Oh*, that's right. Of course."

Outside the closed door, there was the muted sound of nurses talking at the front desk. Someone laughed; a phone rang. Marley took a deep breath. All morning, she'd been trying to keep her mind where it belonged—on being present in the moment. But as hard as she'd been trying, she kept coming right back to Owen again.

Frances seemed to notice. She took her glasses off and set her magazine down. "Is everything okay?"

Marley nodded quickly. "I'm good. Just a little nervous."

It was the appointment where they'd find out the baby's sex, but Dr. Binky would also be looking for normal growth and development today, too, and that made her anxious. She loved this little peanut so much. More than anything, she just wanted this appointment over with so she could stop worrying. So she could stop thinking about Owen missing it. Or wondering if he would've wanted to come if she'd asked.

She chewed the inside of her cheek and thought

about what he'd said the other night in her foyer. The night he'd come to tell her about the workout in Seattle. *I thought you'd give me a chance...* What had he meant by that?

"It's going to be just fine," her foster mother said. "The baby is going to be fine. But I'm not sure that's what's bothering you right now."

Marley looked down.

"Come on," Frances said, leaning forward in her chair. "You've been like this since you stopped seeing Owen."

"We were never really seeing each other..."

"Okay. Since you stopped being friends."

"We're still friends. *But* he's not exactly speaking to me at the moment, so there's that."

"Why isn't he speaking to you?"

She pinched the hem of her gown between her thumb and fingers. "I think I hurt him. I keep pushing him away. But we wouldn't work. He has to know that."

"It could work. You never know."

"Maybe with some other career, but baseball?" She shook her head. "Frances, he'd be gone all the time. Even in the off-season, there are training camps, all kinds of things to keep him away."

"Would you move to be with him? Have you thought about that?"

"I'm not going to leave you. I just got on with the Tiger Sharks... And you know what?" She swallowed hard. "I really like being home again. I wasn't sure I would, with all the memories of my dad, but I do. It's a good place to raise a baby, and now Stella and Kyla are here, too. I can't leave. There's more to it than just being in love."

"Like whether or not he wants to be a father," Frances said quietly.

"Yes. Like that." Again, she thought of what he'd said about wanting a chance. A chance for what? Was he starting to come around to the baby? Or was he simply thinking out loud about a hypothetical relationship with her? Throwing out a statement that wasn't rooted in reality.

She reined herself in. It didn't matter anyway, because he was already gone. The Mariners would like what they saw—there was no doubt about that. When he came back to Christmas Bay, it would be to finish out the season and get ready for the next step in his career.

The door opened, and they turned to see Dr. Binky walk in.

"Well, Marley," he said. "It's nice to see you again. And who's this?"

Frances reached out a hand, not waiting for an introduction. "Frances O'Hara," she said, smiling up at him. "I was lucky enough to help raise Marley. And now I get to be a nana."

Dr. Binky shook her hand. "It's nice to meet you. I'm sure you must be so excited."

"Oh, you don't know the half of it, Doctor. I'm

learning to crochet so I can make a blanket for this little angel. I just need to know if it should be pink or blue."

"Well, you came to the right place, then."

Marley felt a little better. Maybe things would be okay, like Frances said. Maybe she just needed to have faith.

But as Dr. Binky got his stethoscope out and pressed it to her heart, she wondered if it sounded as broken as it felt.

Owen walked behind the brunette with the mile-long legs, trying to pay attention as she pointed out various memorabilia in the Mariners Hall of Fame, a cool little museum right inside the gates of T-Mobile Park.

He should've been in the zone, loving every second of this. But ever since his plane had landed in Seattle, he'd been distracted. Somewhere else. His head definitely wasn't in the game, like his coach had warned against before leaving Christmas Bay.

"You've been different lately," he'd said, taking Owen by the shoulders. "I need you to focus now. This is your shot, Taylor."

Owen had nodded, gritting his teeth. This *was* his shot. And he wanted nothing more than to make his coach proud. To make his teammates and fans proud, too. But he simply couldn't stop thinking about Marley and where they'd left things. With that kiss…

Now he stood in front of a statue of Alex Rodriguez. Looking up at it, but not really seeing it.

"Obviously, one of the greatest in Mariners' history," the brunette said.

He rubbed the back of his neck. She'd been given the job of being his tour guide this afternoon. He felt sorry for her; he wasn't very good company. And for the life of him, he couldn't remember her name. What an asshole.

"No doubt," he said.

She smiled. "I think you might be a little bored."

He opened his mouth to argue, but she held up a hand.

"That's okay," she said. "I don't blame you. They like the PR department to give tours to all the prospective players, and I think it's their idea of wining and dining them. Without the wining. Or the dining."

He laughed, and some of the tension eased from his shoulders for the first time in a week. The workout had gone well. Actually, it had gone amazingly well. He'd thrown like he was on fire. Fastballs, curveballs, any kind of ball they could anticipate— and some they couldn't. He'd known the coaches were impressed, and the guys on the team had been really cool. It had been a good day.

He looked out the museum window now to an unobstructed view of the Seattle skyline. The city was misty today, the Space Needle rising up to pierce a steel-gray sky. Beyond that, Mount Rainier and the

Cascade Range were almost violet-blue, a color he wasn't sure he'd ever seen before in nature.

He'd been treated like a celebrity these last few days, the recruiter doing his best to sell him not only on the team but the city itself. Everything from the sparkling nightlife to the camping, hiking and fishing. But if anything was going to get him pumped about the Mariners, it was the ballpark itself. A state-of-the-art retractable roof stadium, able to seat over forty-seven thousand people. The field was a blend of Kentucky bluegrass and perennial rye, and when he'd stepped onto it for the first time, his cleats sinking into the soft, rich carpet, he thought he might've been dreaming.

But here he was. Standing in its museum, getting a personal tour from its PR department. In reality, he was just an over-the-hill pitcher from their farm team on the coast. But he'd also thrown a ninety-nine-mile-per-hour fastball last night. So, there was that.

The brunette looked at her watch, and he frowned, racking his brain for her name. *Katie, Caddie…*

"You know," she said, "it's just about time for dinner. If you're hungry, I'm free. There's this great Thai restaurant near Pike Place Market…" She smiled at him, and there was something in her eyes that he recognized. He remembered what Marley said about women throwing themselves at him. He wouldn't call this *throwing* by any stretch, but there was definitely something there.

He smiled back. "I've got an early flight in the morning."

"It can't be early enough to justify turning in at five o'clock." She winked. "Come on. I know you've got more questions about Seattle, about this team. I could answer them over a beer. And then you'll be on your way. Until we see each other next time."

He put his hands in his pockets. "You think there'll be a next time, huh?"

"Oh, I think there will be. That arm of yours? Come on."

He let out a long breath. This was what he'd come up here for, after all. To work out with the team, to ask questions, to experience the city. He couldn't really experience the city from the Hyatt Regency...

"Okay," he said. "If you don't have anything else going on."

"Hey. It's my job."

That was officially true, and he was too tired to argue anyway. Thai food on the water sounded good. A beer sounded even better. And if thoughts of Marley kept creeping back in? He'd just have to shut them out again.

*Focus.* That was what his coach had said. And that was just what he intended to do.

Cassie. That was her name. He'd remembered as they were walking through the parking lot, her heels clicking on the cement.

He'd been listening to her talk about the stadium and how the Mariners had just announced a fifty-five-million-dollar renovation. He'd listened to her talk about some of the players and her coworkers in PR. And as they stepped out of her sleek black car and walked into the Thai restaurant overlooking the choppy sapphire waters of Elliott Bay, she began easing away from talking about baseball altogether.

By the time the hostess sat them at a table by the window, he knew she was single. That she was twenty-seven and had graduated from the University of Washington. Working for the Mariners had been her dream all through college, so she could identify on some level how badly he wanted to play in the majors. She'd said this with a little laugh and a toss of her long dark hair. And then the server had brought them their drinks.

Owen took a long swallow of his beer now, staring out the window at the swirling orange-and-purple sunset. It reminded him of the sunsets in Christmas Bay and how the colors bled into the ocean in a perfect mixture of sky and earth. Most nights, it was hard to tell where the sky ended and the water began.

Cassie took a sip of her wine, then set it down on a little cocktail napkin. He could smell the subtle scent of her perfume. She'd taken off her blazer and had a sheer white blouse on underneath. There was a simple strand of pearls around her throat and a pair of small diamond studs in her earlobes. They sparkled underneath the dim restaurant lighting.

Smiling at him, she leaned forward and put her elbows on the table. "You know, I wasn't lying when I said this is all part of my job. But I don't know that I've ever enjoyed it this much before. You're not like most ball players."

"Oh yeah?"

"Mmm-hmm."

"How so?"

"Well, for one thing, you don't seem like a jerk."

Now, that was one he hadn't heard before. He smiled and ran his thumb over the condensation on his mug. It left a clear trail on the foggy glass. Most women, at one time or another, had accused him of being a jackass. Or, at least, they had up until recently. Until Marley had started making him feel like something other than a walking earned run average. She'd actually used the word *sweet* not too long ago. *Sweet.* Him, of all people.

He couldn't help but think that six months ago, a dinner like this might've gone very differently. Back then, he would've recognized the look in Cassie's eyes and wouldn't have thought twice about taking advantage of it. If she was interested, well then, so was he. They probably would have ended up in bed, and then he wouldn't have called her the next day. Claiming to have lost her number and avoiding her if he saw her at the park.

All this because he'd been so scared of falling for someone that he'd done everything humanly possible not to get too close. It was that same old pro athlete cliché. The one that said if any kind of commitment might be required on his part, he'd cut and run. Because he was too serious about his career, about the game, to let anything come between it and him.

And that had made him a complete dick.

He looked up at Cassie. She was beautiful. And she was interested. "You don't know me very well," he said quietly.

She didn't seem put off by this. In fact, she leaned even closer. Until her blouse gaped open, creating a tempting view of her cleavage. "But I like what I see."

There was nothing to say to that. He sure as hell wasn't going to argue. So he took another swallow of his beer. At this rate, he'd have a hangover in the morning, and that was the last thing he needed.

She waited a few seconds, watching him. "I'm sorry," she finally said. "Am I being too forward? I should've asked if you were single, but I just assumed since you're not wearing a ring, and you never mentioned a girlfriend…"

"No, no. That's okay. I'm single."

Saying that didn't feel right. In fact, it felt like broken glass moving over his vocal cords. But it was the truth. He *was* single. He and Marley were…they were… Hell. He had no idea what they were.

Frustrated, he pushed his beer away. He was already in a weird headspace. Adding alcohol to the mix was a dumb idea.

"Have you ever been to Seattle before?" Cassie asked. "You're going to love it, believe me. The weather takes a little getting used to, but that's what the roof over the stadium is for."

He smiled. "That's assuming I'm coming here."

"I can't imagine they wouldn't pick you up, Owen. Especially after this weekend. I don't think you have anything to worry about."

"Even if they do pick me up," he said evenly, "I might not come."

She blinked at him, her long lashes casting a shadow over her cheeks. "What do you mean?"

Opening up to a complete stranger about his personal life wasn't exactly his style. But for some reason, not saying anything at all felt like a betrayal of the situation. Like he was covering it up to keep his career safe. To keep himself safe. And all of a sudden, he was sick of not talking about it.

"I'm going to be a dad," he said.

She watched him and leaned back in her chair. "Oh."

"It wasn't planned," he said. "It was a surprise to us both. I'm still getting used to the idea, to be honest."

"I'm sure you are. It's a big deal."

"It is."

"So, what you're saying is you might not come to Seattle because of the baby?"

"I'm saying I might not come for a lot of reasons."

She nodded, looking down at her wineglass. "I have to tell you, I don't see that very often in this business."

"See what?"

"Hesitation."

He would bet she didn't. Who in their right mind would turn down an opportunity like this? But the reality was complicated. He'd started out thinking that distance from the baby and Marley would be the best thing. That it would protect them from all of his BS and insecurities. But he simply wasn't the same person he'd been a few months ago.

"I never thought I'd say this," he said, "but baseball just doesn't seem as important as it did before. I mean, I love it—don't get me wrong. It's what I've always wanted to do, ever since I can remember. It got me through a tough childhood. It sent me to college. It gave me meaning where I didn't have any before. But now…"

She smiled, her dark hair falling over one eye. "You're growing up."

He let that settle. Then smiled back. "I guess. Yeah. And that's saying something for the oldest guy on the team."

"Can I ask you something?" she said. "For no other reason than I'm curious now?"

He took a sip of his beer, then set it down, licking the tanginess from his lips. "Shoot."

"How do you feel about the baby's mother?"

He waited to answer, but not because he didn't know. He'd known that very first day, when he'd seen her standing next to the field in her businessy clothes, with those buttons all the way to her chin. He loved Marley. He loved everything about her. They were going to have a baby together. In what world didn't he at least try and make that work?

"You don't have to answer that," Cassie said quietly. "I can tell."

Warmth crept up his neck. "You can?"

She nodded.

"I really wasn't prepared for this," he said. "I wasn't going to let anything get in my way…"

"And now you've figured out there's more to life than baseball."

He laughed. "You sound like my buddy. But I wasn't ready to hear it then."

She put her elbows on the table again and leaned forward. But this time she had a very different expression on her face. She looked like a sister or a friend. Or maybe that had everything to do with his mindset—the only woman he wanted was Marley.

"So, Owen Taylor," she said. "Now that you know there's more to life, what are you going to do about it?"

"I guess that depends on whether I get an offer or not. I'll have to decide then."

She lifted her wineglass. "Well, here's to life and major-league baseball. And having the wisdom to separate the two."

He clinked his mug on her glass. "Cheers."

## Chapter Fourteen

Marley picked up the tiny onesie with sea turtles on the front pocket and held it to her cheek. So soft. So sweet. Pretty soon she'd have a little baby to dress in things like this. She could hardly believe a newborn would be this small, but there were a lot of things she couldn't believe. Starting with the fact that she was going to be someone's mother. She was still scared, but the fear was receding more and more, like a wave that left the beach glistening in its wake.

She put the onesie down and looked around the store. Baby bouncers, toys, teething rings, diapers, burp cloths, blankets… There were so many things that came with such a small human being, she had trouble wrapping her head around it. But the shopping was fun.

*You're nesting. A few months early, but still.* That was what Stella had said the other day, making Marley look up from the baby book she'd had her nose in all afternoon.

"I'm what?"

"Nesting," Stella said definitively.

"Oh, I think that's in the next chapter..." She started thumbing through the table of contents.

"It means you're getting ready for the baby," Stella said. "It's instinctual. Most mothers go through it. They paint the baby's room and wash all the little clothes and get everything ready. Do you feel ready?"

Marley had looked up at her again. "Sometimes. But not all the time. Why? Should I feel ready?"

"Not necessarily. But you're definitely nesting. That's a good sign."

Marley smiled now at the memory. She didn't know what she would've done without her foster sisters holding her hand throughout this pregnancy. Without her foster mother's comforting words of wisdom.

And then she felt the smile wilt on her lips. As always, she came back to the same old thought, the same old heartbreak. She just wished Owen was here to share it with her. She wanted him to be walking this path with her. She wanted him to be nervous, too, and making dad jokes about how clueless they were, about how they would struggle through it together.

She'd apparently done too good a job of pushing him away since she hadn't heard from him in a week now. Not since the Mariners workout. And that kiss.

At the thought of his lips on hers, a distinctive warmth crept into her cheeks, and she stiffened, annoyed at herself. She'd gotten what she'd wanted. He was leaving. So, how long would she have to fight this particular battle? Would it always be a part of her life, with their baby a constant and forever reminder of what could have been?

Forcing her shoulders back, she dug the list out of her purse. She needed to be making the most of her day off, not obsessing about Owen. At some point, she needed to let him go. Really let him go. For her sake and for the baby's. No matter how much it hurt, and it would hurt, she needed to say goodbye in her heart.

She looked at the list and swallowed hard. *Wipes, diaper cream, pacifiers*... The layette was almost ready. Now she just needed to put the finishing touches on it. *Definitely* nesting.

Leaning down, she picked up another onesie. This one with animal paw prints all over it. She couldn't seem to get past the PJ aisle, imagining a sleepy little baby in her arms. And she felt an ache in her throat all over again.

Her phone rang from inside her purse, and she pulled it out. *Kyla*...

She swiped her thumb over the screen. "Hey, you," she said, her voice hoarse. "What's up?"

"I just wanted to see if you heard the news about Owen…"

Marley's stomach dropped. She wished time would stop right there. Before she heard anything else. Because, deep down, she already knew what Kyla was about to say. She could feel it in her bones.

"What news?"

"My hairdresser's brother, Max, plays for the Tiger Sharks. He told her that Owen got a call from the Mariners." Kyla paused. "He's going to the show, Marley."

Her foster sister's voice didn't sound light and airy like it usually did over the phone. It sounded sad. Resigned. Because Kyla knew exactly what kind of news this was for Marley.

"When?" she managed. "When did he get the call?"

"Last night."

Marley's heart sank. *Last night.* And he hadn't told her himself. After everything that had happened between them, he hadn't told her.

The realization was sharp as a knife. It wasn't that she hadn't expected him to go—it was that she'd believed they were closer than this. Closer than her having to hear this monumental, life-changing news from anyone other than him.

"Marley?" Kyla said over the phone. "Are you okay?"

"I'm here," she said. "Just processing."

"Do you want me to come get you? We can go for a coffee? Get our toes done?"

It was sweet, but she didn't feel like seeing anyone. All she wanted was to go home and unpack all this. To sort it out in her head and heart.

"I love you," she said quietly. "But I'm all right. I just need to be alone for a while."

"It's going to be okay," Kyla said. "You know that, right?"

Marley smiled, trying to ignore the pain in her chest. It would get better. She just had to give it time. And she had to believe it would.

"Thanks, Kyla. Love you."

"I love you, too."

She hung up as a couple walked by, pushing a cart filled to the brim with baby things. She watched them head down the aisle, the woman's shirt stretched tight over her belly and the man with his hand resting on the small of her back.

She bit the inside of her cheek, missing Owen so badly right then, she ached. She missed his presence and how he made her feel—safe, loved, secure. She missed the peanuts after the games. The talks. The laughter. The bond...

She put the onesie with the paw prints on it in her cart. Then tossed the sea turtle onesie on top of it. Kyla was right. No matter how much she missed Owen, and she'd probably always miss him on some level, it would be okay. She and the baby would be okay. Together, they'd build a life. They'd build a family.

Just the two of them.

Owen cut the motor and sat back in his seat, listening to the lake water lapping at the boat's aluminum underbelly.

He breathed deeply, pulling the mountain air into his lungs. It smelled like pine, like dampness and moss. He took off his Tiger Sharks baseball cap and tilted his head back. The sun was warm on his face, and he closed his eyes, reveling in the moment. Letting the peacefulness seep into his body, his pores, his bones, as a speedboat droned like a bee in the distance.

He'd needed this. He'd needed it for weeks, and now that he was out here, he realized how much weight he'd been carrying around, day in and day out. Not just recently, since he'd found out about the baby. And not since Marley had come into his life. Before that, way before.

He opened his eyes and looked out over the water. The morning sunlight danced over the small swells, creating a cacophony of golden sparkles that looked like flashes from a thousand cameras. It made him think of the press. It made him think of the stadium lights over the field and how their brilliance lingered behind his eyes long after he'd leave the park at night.

He ran a hand through his hair. He'd always measured his success in terms of money, fame, records being broken. And baseball had been a means to that end. It was a way to make something of himself, even though his father never believed he would. And he had. Mostly, he felt like he had. But recently? Recently, his life had shifted in a way that had forced him to reevaluate everything. Especially his definition of success. And his definition of happiness, too.

Ever since stepping off the plane from Seattle, he'd been upside down, inside out. He'd been thinking about his future, his past and everything in between. And his thoughts, chaotic and wild, had always led him back to the same place: Marley.

For him, she was where things began and where they ended. Baseball was baseball. A love of his, for sure. But was it the love of his life? He was starting to feel like it had led him *to* the love of his life. And he'd always be grateful for that.

The sound of the speedboat grew closer, and he looked over to see it making sharp turns on the lake's choppy surface. There were several people on board, laughing, holding drinks in their hands, barely hanging on as the boat bounced over waves created by its own wake.

He watched, thinking of his childhood and how being out here with his dad was the only thing that had ever bonded them. And then even that bond had withered and died through coldness and neglect. Through no fault of his own. But that was the problem—he'd blamed himself for so long, he'd started to believe he didn't deserve good stuff. And maybe that was why he'd self-sabotaged in college, washing out before he'd really gotten started. And maybe that was why he'd been trying to sabotage things now, telling himself he wouldn't be a good father, couldn't be a good father—because of the example that was set for him.

It was bullshit. All of it. He'd finally come to see that on the night he'd gotten home from Seattle. He'd walked in the door to find his house dark and cold. Lonely. That was the word that had risen to the surface of his thoughts. *Lonely.*

He'd turned on a single light, sat down on the couch and looked up at his mantel full of baseball stuff, feeling so empty he wanted to cry for the first time since the day his mother died. That was the moment things had started to change.

He'd gone to practice the next day, played a game that night and had gone back home again. Thinking. Feeling. Letting himself experience the metamorphosis that he knew was happening in his heart. He kept trying to imagine his life from every single angle. Major-league baseball player. Minor-league baseball player. Father. Husband. Bachelor… He imagined it so much that he could actually see his future just as clearly as he could see his past. He could feel the chilliness from a life on the road. In the spotlight—famous but not having anyone in his life who truly knew him. And he could feel the warmth of a life with a family. In a small town that he'd come to care for, despite all the sad things that had happened there. He could feel it all. And he weighed it all, day and night, for a solid week.

And then the Mariners had called.

He sat in his boat now, feeling the sunlight on his shoulders, breathing in the scent of the mountains and the ocean in the distance. He'd made a decision last night after having a long, heartfelt talk with his coach and had come out here this morning to let it settle. And to figure out how he was going to tell Marley. He knew she'd have trouble with it, no matter what she'd said before or how she tried to present herself to the world—tough and independent, someone who could and would do it on her own. He knew she'd have things to say, if not right away, then someday soon. And he'd just have to cross that bridge when he came to it.

Pulling his phone from his pocket, he brought up Marley's number and typed a message out. Short and sweet. He didn't need to go into everything right now. They could talk about it later. As soon as she agreed to see him. Just like he'd needed time this morning to let it settle, so would she.

Letting out a breath he hadn't realized he'd been holding, he put his phone back in his pocket and leaned over for his fishing pole. He'd spend an hour or so on the water, and then he'd head back into town to get ready for the game tonight.

The hum of the speedboat grew closer, higher pitched, and the breeze picked up, leaving chills on the back of his neck. He looked over again to see that it was headed in his direction.

He watched it for a few seconds, waiting for it to peel off to the left or right. Or slow down. Or do anything really, other than roar toward his little boat that was rocking so gently on the water.

He stood, working to keep his balance. But still, it kept coming. He waved his hand in the air. Then waved both hands in the air, as it continued slicing its way through the water, nobody on board seeming to notice him at all.

*This could actually be bad*, he thought. *Really bad.* He had a fleeting moment of wondering what the hell he was going to do now. It wasn't like there were a lot of options. And then he remembered the air horn in his tackle box, something Max had suggested last summer. Max. Always with the safety first.

But then he realized there wasn't time. He stared at the boat barreling toward him, saw a woman in a bikini frantically tugging on the driver's arm.

He said a prayer and dived in the water.

We need to talk. After the game?

Marley looked at the text again, then sat on her couch, careful not to knock over the clean pile of baby clothes that she'd just folded. She'd read those two little sentences so many times over the last hour that the words had begun to blur on the screen, their possible meaning getting jumbled in her head. He wanted to talk. Why now? Where had he been these last few weeks? Where had he gone after that kiss? After the news from the Mariners? It was true that she was responsible for a good part of this. She'd asked for space, and he'd given it to her. But it also felt like he'd disappeared completely, and that part was hard to swallow.

She'd been so hurt when he'd walked out of the locker room the other night, never even looking up at the announcer's box, that she'd had trouble not crying in front of Tony. But she was pretty sure he knew what was going on by now anyway. He'd patted her awkwardly on the back, reminding her that he'd be ready with his truck whenever she picked out that crib.

She set her phone on the coffee table and rubbed her eyes. It felt like she was being torn in half. A part of her was so desperate for him to stay, so in love with him, that she needed to believe this text meant something.

The other part, the cautious, reasonable, realistic part, couldn't just dismiss how distant he'd become. As her belly had grown and as the baby's kicks had gotten stronger, so had the instinct to protect herself and her child. She thought she and Owen had decided to be friends. And if he wanted to be a part of the baby's life later, even better. But what she couldn't do was let someone in who would crush them later. And this text? This casual reappearance? It seemed like it was coming from someone who might do that. Whether he was trying to or not.

She looked over at the small pile of onesies and rested her hand there. Felt the downy softness underneath her fingertips. *Owen*... She wanted to trust him. But how could she? That was the question that had haunted her from the beginning. How could she trust something that she wanted so badly?

She sat there for a few minutes gazing out the window at the seagulls bobbing on the ocean breeze over the bay where the fishing boats were chugging out to sea. She imagined being on one of them now, being carried away to a place where she was all alone. Just her and the water, the sun and the baby. She imagined what it would be like, just the two of them against the world.

She glanced down at her phone with a sigh. She needed to text him back. But she also needed to figure out what to say first. Prepare herself for how things might look if they talked tonight.

Tucking her hair behind her ears, she grabbed the baby clothes and stood. If she hurried, she could get these put away and take a quick shower before Stella and Frances picked her up for lunch. They'd be able to center her. Help her focus and see things more clearly. They always did.

But before she took a step, her phone rang.

Frowning, she picked it up. A number she didn't recognize flashed across the screen, and she answered with a funny feeling in her stomach.

"Hello?"

"Marley. It's Max."

She froze. Max had never called her before. In fact, she didn't even know he had her number.

"Max? What's going on?"

"Owen's had an accident," Max said, his voice crackly on the other end of the line. "He's at the hospital, but he's unconscious. I called you as soon as I found out. I know he'd want you to know."

Marley put her hand on the couch to steady herself. "How?" she managed. "What happened?"

"He was fishing. I guess another boat hit him. The driver had been drinking."

"Oh my God."

"They'll barely tell me anything over the phone. And he's got no family close by. I guess you and I are the closest thing. I'm headed there now. Do you want me to pick you up on the way?"

She nodded, feeling sick. "Please..."

"He's one tough bastard," Max said. "Try not to worry. He'll be okay."

It was an empty promise. She knew he couldn't say that with any confidence and neither could she. She stood there shaking, an unbearable ache in her chest. She hadn't realized how much she loved him until just that moment. How much she was hoping he'd stay. She simply hadn't let herself go there in her heart, but that was the funny thing about love. It never let you off the hook that easy.

"Thank you," she said. "Thank you for calling me, Max."

The phone line crackled again. She could tell he was standing outside, the wind buffeting the receiver. "He loves you, Marley," he said. "He really does."

She felt herself smile at that.

"I'll be there in ten minutes," he said.

And the line went dead.

## *Chapter Fifteen*

Marley made her way down the sterile white hallway of Christmas Bay General. She'd thought the next time she'd walk through the doors, she'd be getting ready to have the baby. Instead, she was coming to see Owen, wondering how it was that she could've gone this long without telling him how she felt. *Really* felt. Even if he wasn't going to stay, she wanted him to know how deeply she'd fallen in love with him. How clear things were to her now. Pushing him away hadn't been fair. She'd created a wall, meant to protect her from that old pain her father had inflicted. But he wasn't her father. He was a different kind of man altogether, and she'd always love him. No matter what happened between them.

Max walked beside her, his cleats clicking on the

waxed floor. He'd been on the field when he'd gotten the phone call from the police. Apparently, Owen had his number in his wallet.

She could feel him looking over every now and then as they headed toward the ICU, and she could tell he was worried. Tears had been streaming down her cheeks since he'd picked her up, something she couldn't help. They just kept coming, like someone had left the faucet on.

She wiped her eyes now and turned to him, giving him a smile. Wanting to reassure him but feeling like the bottom had dropped out of her world. All she could think about was getting to Owen.

They turned a corner and saw the nurses' station ahead. Doctors were being paged overhead, and an orderly brushed past, pushing a squeaky cart full of medical equipment.

Marley stepped up to the circular desk, just as a nurse fixed her with a stern look. *These are the gatekeepers*, Marley thought. *It might be hard getting past.*

"May I help you?"

"Yes," Marley said. "I'm Marley Carmichael. Our friend was in a boating accident. Owen Taylor? We were hoping we could talk to a doctor?"

The nurse frowned. "Are you family?"

Her stomach sank, and she glanced at Max, who was starting to pace the floor. "No, we're friends."

"Are you his emergency contacts?"

She'd had a feeling this was how it was going to go down. Swallowing hard, she shook her head. "No."

"Does he have family we can contact? And could they relay the information to you?"

"His mom passed away. He has a dad, but they're estranged. I don't think Owen even knows where he is."

The nurse bit her bottom lip, clearly feeling for her but caught between a rock and a hard place. "Can you wait right here? Let me go track my supervisor down. See what we can do, okay?"

"I really appreciate it. Thank you so much."

Marley watched the nurse push away from the desk and disappear down the hallway.

Max sighed. "It seems like they could tell us *something*."

"I know. I'm really hoping they will." She put her hand on her stomach. It was so strange that she was carrying Owen's child, yet on paper, she wasn't even close enough to him to get the most basic information when he was lying unconscious in a hospital bed.

Max stepped close and put an arm around her. "It's gonna be okay. Tough bastard, remember?"

She forced another smile. It was either that or break down.

"Marley?"

She turned to see a nurse in purple scrubs standing behind the desk. She had her red hair pulled into a bun, and something about her looked vaguely familiar.

"Yes?"

"I'm Allie Martin. I know Frances from the shop. I worked there in high school?"

Marley felt her mouth hang open. "Little Allie Martin?"

Allie laughed. "Well, not so little anymore."

"How are you? I didn't know you were back in Christmas Bay."

"I didn't know you were back, either. This place has a pull, doesn't it?"

Marley was beginning to think coming home to Christmas Bay had been her destiny all along. Coming back to Frances. To Stella and Kyla. And now to Owen, too.

Allie looked over her shoulder, then leaned toward them over the desk. "I don't know if they'll end up telling you anything," she said quietly. "The hospital is so strict with their privacy rules. But I know about you and Owen. About the baby. Obviously, you two are close…"

This didn't surprise Marley. Christmas Bay was so small. And Frances had probably let it slip more than once. It was what it was.

"Yes, we are."

Allie's expression fell. "He's lucky to be alive. I guess he saw the other boat coming and was able to jump off in time. But he's got a possible spinal injury, so they're keeping him sedated for now. He needs to be still, and the swelling needs to go down before they'll know for sure. But you should be able to talk to him yourself in a day or so."

Marley let out a shaky breath. *Spinal injury...* The words were terrifying. She couldn't imagine someone as strong and vital as Owen lying so still in a hospital bed. She wondered if he'd been conscious when they'd brought him in. She wondered how much pain he'd been in or if he'd been thinking about his career. His future.

"Thank you, Allie," she said. "It helps to know."

"Of course. Physically, he's in great shape, and that will help him moving forward. Hang in there, okay?"

She nodded. And then Allie was gone, leaving her and Max alone again, the sounds of the ICU enveloping them in its unsettling embrace.

"I've got to call Coach," Max said. "Let him know what's going on."

"Okay..."

Max frowned, looking down at her. "Are you sure you're all right? This must be really stressful for you."

"You're sweet. I'm okay, though. I promise."

Max watched her. He was so young. She knew Owen was more like an older brother to him than just a friend, and worry was etched all over his face.

"You're sure?" he asked.

"Positive."

"Okay. I'll just be outside. Holler if you need anything."

"I will."

With one more look, he finally turned and headed down the hallway, disappearing around the corner.

She walked into the small waiting room but couldn't bring herself to sit. Instead, she stood there staring out the window to the parking lot, her heart knocking painfully in her chest. She needed something to do, some way to help, even if it was small. She worried her bottom lip with her teeth. She knew where Owen's spare key was. Maybe she'd go grab him some extra socks and underwear, his razor and shaving cream... Things from home that would be good to have when he woke up. She had to believe that he'd be okay when he did wake up. She wouldn't, *couldn't*, let herself imagine anything else.

Leaning against the windowsill, she watched the ever-present seagulls overhead. They dipped and bobbed on the breeze, their small gray-and-white bodies graceful as dancers against the periwinkle sky. They'd always been such a constant presence for her growing up here that she wondered what she'd ever done without them. Without the ocean. Without the town itself.

She thought about Owen then and how he'd settled back in Christmas Bay, too. Coming home seemed to have been as easy for him as slipping on an old glove. Whether he knew it or not, it fit. That didn't mean another town, another city, wouldn't fit, too, but it wouldn't be the *same* fit.

Exhausted, she finally sank down near the coffee maker and wrapped her arms around herself. When Max came back, she'd ask him to take her home so she could get her car and go get Owen's things. Then she'd sleep here tonight if she could find a chair comfortable enough for her back. Owen wouldn't know the difference, but she didn't care. She just wanted to be close.

"We can close the shop," Stella said over the phone, "and come down there to sit with you."

Marley flipped on her blinker and slowed as Owen's street came into view. Her heart broke as she pictured pulling up to his house that very first night. They'd had no idea what they'd been about to set in motion when he'd unzipped that little black dress. They'd just been acting on instinct. On pure, natural attraction.

She gripped the steering wheel tighter, feeling the seat belt stretch over her swollen belly. Her love for Owen and fear for his future brought fresh tears to her eyes.

"No," she said. "Don't do that. Frances would only worry. It's better for her to stay busy."

Stella sighed on the other end of the line. "*I'm* going to worry."

"I know. But I'll be okay. Max will be there. And the coach and his wife. And his teammates have been coming and going, so I'm definitely not alone."

"Poor Owen." Marley could picture her foster sister shaking her head, her pretty face drawn. "And there's no update?"

"They won't tell me much. But there's not much to tell right now anyway. He's still asleep. I think he'll have an MRI when they wake him up, and then we'll know more."

"Okay. I still think we should come down there to be with you…"

"Try not to worry. I'll call you tonight and let you know how it's going. I love you."

"Love you, too."

Marley hung up just as she was pulling up to Owen's house. Her shoulders and neck were stiff with tension, and she had a headache throbbing at her temples.

She put the car into Park and sat there for a minute looking over at his house. How long would it be before he was home again? She hoped and prayed it would be soon. But at the same time, she knew she had to prepare herself for a different outcome. Something more painful. And her throat ached.

Turning the engine off, she opened the door into the stiff breeze. It immediately snatched at her hair, blowing it in front of her face. She pushed it back and made her way to the front door.

Owen kept his spare key in the most obvious place ever, underneath a rock painted like a baseball. She'd given him a hard time about it at the beginning of the summer. *Now I know where your key is. What if I just let myself in?* He'd smiled that trademark smile. The one that could light up a room. *That's a chance I'm willing to take*, he'd said with a wink.

Her heart twisted now as she knelt down to pick it up. When she'd thought about coming over to grab a few things, she hadn't been thinking of how hard it would be. Of how much emotion she'd have to fight back, simply by walking through his door.

Straightening, she unlocked the dead bolt and stepped inside the entryway. She stood there for a minute, concentrating on her breathing. *In, out...in, out...* His scent lingered in the air. A mixture of his deodorant and aftershave, leather and sunscreen...

Light-headed, she looked around. The house was spotless. Gone were the piles of workout clothes on the couch, the cleats on the floor, the Diet Coke cans on the kitchen counter. It actually looked like a grown-up lived here.

Marley felt a smile stretch across her lips, the first genuine one in hours. He'd asked her once if his sloppiness bothered her, and she'd told him the truth—she was a neat freak. He'd smiled and nodded, and hadn't said another word. She couldn't presume he'd done this for her, but she couldn't help but wonder if he had.

She stood there with her hand on her belly and, for a few seconds, allowed herself to imagine something she never had before. She allowed herself to picture them together.

Looking around, she saw herself snuggled beside him on the couch. She saw him walking up behind her and wrapping his arms around her at the kitchen counter. She saw herself making coffee in the mornings and him pacing the floor with a fussy baby. She saw an Exersaucer in the corner and bottles in the refrigerator. She saw family here. She saw happiness here.

And then she remembered why she'd come. The warm feeling eased from her chest like a blanket being pulled away. The question of whether or not he intended to be a father to this baby wasn't the only question now. There were so many more. Like, how would he recover from this accident? And how would he feel afterward, after coming so close to not surviving? Marley knew that kind of experience could change a person. As it should.

Taking a breath, she looked around one more time. Then made her way down the hallway.

The house was so quiet, she could hear the low hum of the air-conditioning unit through the vents. The cool air moved over her skin, leaving goose bumps on her arms. There was the faint, tangy smell of paint as she passed the guest bedroom, and she looked over to see the door wide open.

And then she stopped in her tracks.

There, in the far corner of the room, was a crib. Marley felt herself staring. As if blinking might make it disappear.

*A crib*. He'd bought a crib. But not only that, he'd painted. He'd bought diapers. There were two boxes stacked neatly in the corner.

She leaned against the wall and shook her head. He hadn't said a word. This whole time she'd been wondering if he'd eventually come around to being a dad. And little did she know, he'd been coming around this whole time. In his own way. Probably slowly. Very slowly, but he'd come around enough to make a nursery.

*A nursery...*

Her heart squeezed. She hadn't thought she could love Owen any more than she already did. But this wasn't the first time he'd surprised her. She knew buying baby things didn't mean he wouldn't change his mind. Of course he could. And it didn't mean he'd be a good dad or even a present dad. But it meant he wanted to try, and that meant so much to her. More than he could ever know.

She stood there looking at the room. Wanting to hug him, kiss him. And then, slowly, reality crept back in, and she remembered again why she was here. Owen was unconscious in a hospital bed. There was swelling around his spine. He'd almost been killed.

She bit her lip so hard she thought she could taste blood. Frances would say this was one of life's curveballs. But she had to keep reminding herself that Owen could hit anything.

Owen was still groggy. His eyes felt heavy and his vision was blurred. But the doctors had just told him not to worry, that it would pass.

Since he'd woken up, he'd been told a lot of things he was still trying to process. Mainly that he'd been kept sedated so the swelling in his back and neck would go down. He'd been taken for an MRI, and it had confirmed what his doctor had initially hoped for. Soft tissue damage to the ligaments, but nothing that wouldn't heal with time and some physical therapy. No spinal fractures. No break of any kind.

Owen was possibly the luckiest son of a bitch who ever lived. At least, that was what he kept telling himself as one of his nurses fussed with the settings on his bed. They'd transferred him to a regular room this morning, something more relaxed and comfortable (their words, not his), but he couldn't wait to get the hell out of here. To get up and put his clothes on and find Marley. That was all he'd been thinking about for the last hour. *Marley, Marley, Marley...* Finding her. Telling her what he'd been planning on telling her before his fishing interlude went very, very wrong.

He closed his eyes against the sunlight that was filtering in through the blinds. He had a massive headache, but he'd refused any more pain meds. He'd wait on those until after he'd talked to Marley. He wanted his head to be clear, his thoughts to be concise and linear. He needed this to make sense to her since it might be the most important conversation he'd ever had in his life.

"Oh, is that too bright?" the nurse asked, closing the blinds. Her name was Vanessa, according to her name tag.

He felt swimmy, out of it, but he wanted to see Marley so badly that he forced himself to sit up a little, which was a mistake. Pain screamed through his shoulder, and he winced.

Vanessa the nurse frowned and fluffed the pillow behind his neck. "You'd really be more comfortable if you'd let us give you something."

"I will," he said. "But I want to see my girlfriend first."

"We called her, but it went straight to voice mail. The nurses out front said she was here most of the night. I'm sure she'll be back soon. She probably went home to shower or get something to eat."

Looking up at her, he forced a smile. He had to assume she knew what she was talking about. She dealt with patients and their families every day. Still, it was hard not to be impatient. He'd lost his damn phone at the bottom of the lake, and he had no way of tracking her down himself.

*Patients and their families...* He let those words seep into his consciousness like honey on a warm piece of toast. *Family.* Was that what Marley was to him? He didn't have to think long on that to know the answer. She was. She and the baby were his family. He hadn't had one in a very long time, and never a completely functional one. But he had one now. If she wanted the same thing.

He looked over at the open door, suddenly so anxious he wasn't sure he'd be able to take another minute of fluffing pillows and getting his blood pressure taken. He just wanted Marley.

And then, there she was.

She appeared in the doorway like an apparition, wide-eyed and out of breath. Her cheeks were flushed pink, and he thought how good that looked on her. How good pregnancy looked on her.

He saw her then, the way she'd been as a girl. In her baggy clothes with that wild blond hair hanging in her face. Sitting high on the bleachers at his games—sad, quiet, alone. She'd been beautiful then, but he hadn't known enough about life or about himself to see past all her layers.

He could see past them now. He could see straight to her heart.

"Owen?" she said quietly.

He smiled. He'd missed her so much. So damn much.

Vanessa nodded at her and brushed past, leaving her standing in the doorway watching him.

He patted the bed. "Come here."

She stepped inside the room, and he caught her scent. Light, flowery, sweet. She was wearing a dress today, something yellow and flowy. It draped across her stomach like a soft hug.

"My phone died," she said. "I went home to grab my charger, and I missed a call from the hospital. I was so happy when I heard it, I couldn't get here fast enough…"

He reached for her hand. Her long tapered fingers wrapped around his. They were beautiful, just like the rest of her.

"I hope you didn't speed," he said. "I don't know what I'd do if anything happened to you."

She swallowed visibly. "How do you feel?"

"I'm okay. Bruises, sore back. Pulled some muscles and ligaments, but no lasting damage. I'll be fine."

Exhaling, she sagged against the bed. "Thank God."

"I got lucky. I need to go buy a lottery ticket or something."

"Or something."

"Sit," he said. "We need to talk."

She sat down beside him. Her shoulders were freckled and brown. She'd gotten some sun. He could see it in her face, in the apples of her cheeks, where there were some freckles, too. She was stunning. She was going to be a mother. And he knew she was going to be an amazing one.

She looked down at him, and it seemed like there was something she might want to say, too. Maybe they both had something to say.

He took a deep breath, his hand resting on her thigh. He rubbed his thumb lightly over the fabric of her dress, thinking of the night they'd spent together. She'd been wearing a very different kind of dress then. He remembered how he'd slipped it over her head and how her naked body had looked in the moonlight. He'd never seen such perfection before. And now she was carrying his child. How had he gotten so lucky?

But there was more to their relationship than the

baby between them. Much more. In order to have some kind of future, there would need to be trust between them. And that meant she'd have to believe him when he told her what he'd been wanting to since the morning of his accident.

"Marley," he began. "Do you trust me?"

She stared down at him, her lips slightly parted. But instead of saying anything, she simply nodded.

"Good," he said. "Because I'm going to need you to have faith in me. I'm going to need you to believe me when I say what I need to say."

"I'll believe you," she said.

Letting his gaze drop to her belly, he moved his hand there. He felt how warm it was and imagined the baby, safe in her womb.

She put her hand over his.

"I've always loved baseball," he said quietly. "I have it to thank for every good thing in my life."

"Me too," she said.

"It's made me happy when I didn't think I could be happy again. It gave me a future when nobody thought I'd have one. Including my own father."

His voice broke a little then, and she squeezed his hand. But she stayed quiet, and he was glad. If she'd said anything right then, he didn't think he'd be able to get through the rest of this. And he needed to. For both of them.

"For a long time," he continued, "I thought that to be a success, I would have to be playing ball. It's the only thing I really know how to do. I mean, I wasn't a great student. But I could always throw a ball. I could always do that really well."

Her lovely green eyes grew misty. It hadn't been his intention to make her cry. But he wanted to be honest with her. As honest as he'd ever been with anyone before. And he needed her to believe him.

"The thought of *not* being a ball player scared me," he said. "Because that seemed like the only thing keeping me from turning into my dad. But when I saw you again after so long…"

He swallowed hard. This was where it was supposed to get easier. The easy part should've been telling her how he felt about her. How she'd changed the way he looked at his life.

But he realized that telling her how he felt, being completely open with her, meant he was blazing a new trail. He felt like a clumsy little boy trying to juggle a Fabergé egg, and he noticed then that his hands were actually shaking.

Marley reached out and ran her fingertips along his jawline. Her fingers felt like butterfly wings on his skin.

She waited, watching him. Trusting him, just like he'd asked her to.

"When I met you again, when we reconnected," he said, "all that changed. When you got pregnant, I started to see myself through your eyes. Through our baby's eyes. And I'm more than just a ball player."

She smiled then. And it was radiant. "Yes," she said. "You are."

"It took me a while to know what it is that I really want. I needed time to sit with this, to be with it. The morning of the accident, I texted you because I wanted to tell you that I know now. I know what I want."

Marley let out a visible breath. She probably thought she knew by now what he was about to say. She probably thought he was going to try being a dad from Seattle. That maybe they could make a relationship work, too. And that was what he'd been thinking as well. Up until a few days ago. A few days ago, everything had changed in his mind, in his heart. When he'd decided to stay in Christmas Bay.

"I'm not going to play for the Mariners," he said evenly.

Her expression, which had been one of quiet contemplation, of knowing, at least on some level, changed then. Her eyebrows knitted together, and her lips tilted down at the sides. She looked worried. Confused. And she leaned away.

"What?" she said.

"I'm not leaving."

"What are you talking about? You have to leave. This is the chance of a lifetime."

"No," he said. And palmed her belly with a possessiveness that took him by surprise. "*This* is the chance of a lifetime. Baseball is just a game, Marley."

"Owen," she said, shaking her head, "I can't let you do this. We can talk about us. We can make it work from a distance."

"We could talk about it, sure. And we could try

to make it work. And maybe I could even convince you at some point to follow me up there. But I know that's not what you want. Your family is here. Frances needs you, and I wouldn't ask you to leave."

"I can't ask you to stay."

"You're not asking me. I'm telling you. And this isn't because of the accident. I'd made up my mind before that. This is what I wanted to talk to you about. This is what I wanted to tell you."

She looked away and stared across the room, her expression unreadable now. And that worried him.

"Hey," he said.

She looked back at him.

"Talk to me."

She frowned, shifting on the bed. "I think you're going to end up resenting me for this. Or you'll resent the baby."

"Hey." This time his voice was firm, solid. She was trying to run from this. Just like he'd run his entire life, but he wasn't going to let her. Not if he could help it. "You said you'd trust me, remember?"

She nodded.

"This is what trusting me looks like. This wasn't an overnight decision, Marley. Hell, I don't even think it was a decision I made this summer. I think it might even go farther back than that. I haven't let myself want a family before, and you know why. If this baby hadn't been a surprise, I might never have had the guts to do this."

"But walk away from baseball? That's crazy. It's your life."

"It's part of my life, but it's not my whole life. And I wouldn't be walking away."

"You'd keep playing for the Tiger Sharks?"

"No. I'd be coaching the Tiger Sharks."

Her green eyes widened.

He smiled, enjoying this part. She'd had no idea this was a possibility. And truthfully, neither had he. But around the time he'd found out about the workout in Seattle, his coach had brought him into his office and closed the door. He'd told Owen he was moving up. He'd been hired as a batting coach for the Diamondbacks. He and his family were moving to Arizona this fall.

Owen had tucked this away and chewed on it for days. The head coaching job would be wide open. He was young and had a lot to learn, but he was also damn good at baseball and knew a lot of people. He had strings he could pull. He could probably make it work if he wanted to. And then, when he'd stepped off the plane from Seattle, he knew he'd wanted to. It was as simple as that.

He never thought he could have it all. He never thought he deserved it. But now here he was, making plans for his future, which included a family. And feeling an excitement in his bones that he hadn't felt in a very long time.

Now he just had to convince Marley to take this leap with him. To trust him.

He took her hand in his. "Say something, baby."

Her expression gave him some hope. She wanted this. He knew she did. She was just afraid, and he understood that.

"I don't want to let myself believe you," she said quietly.

"I know. But having faith doesn't just mean having faith when things are easy. It means having faith when they're hard, too. And this is hard. But I'm asking you to trust it, Marley. I'm asking you to look at me, and see that you're the best thing that's ever happened to me."

"Owen…" she whispered.

"Not everyone is going to leave," he said. He reached out and cupped her cheek in his hand, running his thumb underneath her eyelashes. "*I'm* not going to leave you."

She smiled, and for the first time since walking through the door, it was easy and true. It was like the sun coming out from behind a cloud. For him, it was everything.

"I love you," she said. "I just love you so much."

He rested his hand on her stomach again and thought he felt the faintest kick. It was possible their baby knew exactly what they were saying, what they were feeling in that moment. After all, it had brought them together in the first place and had lit the brightest, hottest fire.

"Did you feel that?" he asked. "I think this kid is

going to follow in his old man's footsteps. He's going to play baseball, and he's gonna be amazing at it."

Marley's smile grew wider, more stunning, if that was possible. She leaned in and kissed him, and she tasted like summer. Like Coke and peanuts. She felt like the sun on the back of his neck. Like a home run and tender spring grass underneath his feet.

She felt like a dream come true.

"*She's* going to be amazing at it," she murmured. And kissed him again.

## *Epilogue*

Marley pulled her knit cap down over her ears and shifted on the bleachers. She'd remembered to bring a stadium cushion to sit on, but her back was still aching. Only a few more weeks to go, but Dr. Binky had told her it could be anytime now since she was already dilated a centimeter. Plus, she kept having random contractions, something he'd said was completely normal, but she wondered about the timing just the same.

Rubbing her stomach, she looked across the field to where Owen was giving his second lesson of the afternoon. He was firmly entrenched in the off-season now, with Christmas on the horizon, but his private pitching lessons had taken off, and he was busier than ever.

They'd laughed about it over dinner last night,

joking that he could probably be making more as a personal coach. But the money didn't matter—his heart belonged to minor-league baseball. *Well,* he'd said, taking another bite of pizza, *minor-league baseball and you.*

She watched him now, her heart squeezing. He was so handsome, so tall and fit, that the sight of him still gave her butterflies. He'd walk into the house, the house they now shared, and she'd catch herself staring. She couldn't help it. By now she'd gotten used to the pregnancy hormones, the ones that had intensified her libido and made it embarrassingly hard to concentrate on anything else. But she knew she couldn't blame the hormones for this. She was simply in love. And with the baby so close now, she was truly happy for the first time in her life.

Owen looked over at her. She knew he was worried about her coming out today and sitting in the cold. But she loved watching him with the kids. It gave her a sense of peace that she hadn't realized she'd been missing. She'd sat on these same bleachers as a lonely teenager. Frances had given her a home then—she'd given her love and safety. But when Owen had come back into her life again, that last piece of the puzzle had slid into place.

She was finally at peace.

Shifting again, she waved to reassure him. Her hips hurt a little and her lower belly felt oddly tight, but he was almost done. Just giving a few more tips to the high school boy, who kept looking up at him with such awe. Owen had become an absolute treasure in Christmas Bay. People didn't just ask for his autograph anymore—they greeted him by name. Shook his hand. Talked to him about coaching. And the community valued his opinion and his experience, which meant the world to him. She'd watched him grow over the last several months, change. He was coming into his own as a man, as a partner and as a father.

Marley tucked her hands in her pockets as the wind picked up, bringing with it a few stinging drops of rain. She watched him say goodbye to the boy and his dad and then turn to pick up his duffel bag next to the dugout. It had taken her a while, but she'd finally stopped worrying about the future. Wondering if he'd get tired of Christmas Bay or, worse, her and the baby. And she'd started trusting him when he said he was happy. Probably because she could see it in his eyes. This life, this quiet life just shy of the bright lights in those big-league stadiums, suited Owen Taylor, the boy with the golden arm. And it suited her, the girl who'd always watched him from afar.

She looked at her watch. In about an hour, she was going to meet Frances, Stella and Kyla at the shop and then walk down to Mario's for an early dinner. They were going to talk about Frances's house and how much longer she could realistically take care of it, even with help. The old Victorian was the heart of their family, where they'd grown up, where they'd spent birthdays and holidays and summer vacations since they were preteens. It was a hard subject to broach for Marley and her foster sisters, but it was even harder for Frances, who'd spent so many happy years there with Bud.

Marley pulled in a deep breath, letting the salty air fill her lungs before slowly releasing it. This was just another one of life's curveballs. They'd do their best. But at the end of the day, as much as they loved it, the house was just a house, and they'd always have each other.

Reaching over to grab her purse, she felt a sudden warmth spread along her inner thighs. She froze, her heart thumping in her chest. Then looked down to see a dark stain on her jeans.

Shaking, she looked back up to see Owen walking toward her, a smile on his handsome face.

"Ready to go, baby?" he asked. "It's getting cold out here."

She felt herself smile back, her body humming with adrenaline. "I'm ready to go," she said. "To the hospital."

He stopped in his tracks. "What?"

"My water just broke."

He looked down at her jeans, and all the color drained from his face.

She stood with a grunt, and he stumbled up the steps to grab her hand.

"Be careful," he managed. "Can you walk?"

She laughed. "I can walk. Can *you* walk?"

"I don't know. Ask me in thirty seconds."

"We need to stop by the house and get my bag. And call Dr. Binky."

"Bag, Dr. Binky. Got it."

"And Frances. And Stella and Kyla. I was supposed to meet them at the shop…"

"Call the girls," he said, helping her down the steps. "Got it."

She stepped onto the gravel surrounding the field and looked up at Owen. "We're going to have a baby," she said. "We're going to be parents."

His eyes were maybe the bluest she'd ever seen them. He looked scared. He looked excited. But most of all, he looked happy. Really, really happy.

"We're going to be parents," he said, pulling her close. "And I love you."

He said this all the time, but she never got tired of hearing it. In the mornings, he'd roll over in bed, put his arms around her and kiss her temple. And he'd tell her how special she was, how lucky he was to have found her again. In the evenings, he'd walk up behind her and move her hair away from her neck, kissing it sweetly, gently. And he'd tell her then, too.

There was a time when Marley hadn't believed people when they said they loved her. As a girl, she'd pushed Frances away physically, emotionally. Until, after hundreds and hundreds of *I love you*s, Marley finally began believing she was worthy of being loved.

Her foster mother had paved the way for Owen all those years ago, but he'd had to take the first steps on the journey that ended with her heart. And with her daughter's heart.

She smiled as she pulled away, feeling a tightening in her lower belly. A twinge that would soon become more than a twinge. Much more. She was so grateful to those stars aligning nine months ago. Grateful to this little girl who had brought her mom and dad back together—two kids who had started out so unwanted but had ended up in each other's arms. Like it was always meant to be.

Maybe someday, a long, long time from now, their daughter would get to hear the story of how they'd met and fallen in love. Or, at least, part of the story. But until then, she'd simply have to settle for being adored by them both.

"I love you, too," Marley said.

And meant every word.

\* \* \* \* \*

## #2989 THE MAVERICK'S SURPRISE SON
*Montana Mavericks: Lassoing Love* • by Christine Rimmer

Volunteer firefighter Jace Abernathy vows to adopt the newborn he saved from a fire. Nurse Tamara Hanson doubts he's up to the task. She'll help the determined rancher prepare for his social service screening. But in the process, will these hometown heroes find love and family with each other?

## #2990 SEVEN BIRTHDAY WISHES
*Dawson Family Ranch* • by Melissa Senate

Seven-year-old Cody Dawson dreams of meeting champion bull rider Logan Winston. Logan doesn't know his biggest fan is also his son. He'll fulfill seven of Cody's wishes—one for each birthday he missed. But falling in love again with Cody's mom, Annabel, may be his son's biggest wish yet!

## #2991 HER NOT-SO-LITTLE SECRET
*Match Made in Haven* • by Brenda Harlen

Sierra Hart knows a bad boy when she sees one. And smooth-talking Deacon Parrish is a rogue of the first order! Their courtroom competition pales to their bedroom chemistry. But will these dueling attorneys trust each other enough to go from "I object" to "I do"?

## #2992 HEIR IN A YEAR
by Elizabeth Bevarly

Bennett Hadden just inherited the Gilded Age mansion Summerlight. So did Haven Moreau—assuming the two archenemies can live there together for one year. Haven plans to restore the home *and* her broken relationship with Bennett. And she'll use every tool at her disposal to return both to their former glories!

## #2993 THEIR SECRET TWINS
*Shelter Valley Stories* • by Tara Taylor Quinn

Jordon Lawrence and ex Mia Jones just got the embryo shock of their lives. Their efforts to help a childless couple years ago resulted in twin daughters they never knew existed. Now the orphaned girls need their biological parents, and Jordon and Mia will work double time to create the family their children deserve!

## #2994 THE BUSINESS BETWEEN THEM
*Once Upon a Wedding* • by Mona Shroff

Businessman Akash Gupta just bought Reena Pandya's family hotel, ruining her plan to take it over. Now the determined workaholic will do anything to reclaim her birthright—even get closer to her sexy ex. But Akash has a plan, too—teaching one very headstrong woman to balance duty, family *and* love.

---

# Get 4 FREE REWARDS!

**We'll send you 2 FREE Books plus 2 FREE Mystery Gifts.**

**FREE** Value Over **$20**

Both the **Harlequin® Special Edition** and **Harlequin® Heartwarming™** series feature compelling novels filled with stories of love and strength where the bonds of friendship, family and community unite.

---

**YES!** Please send me 2 FREE novels from the Harlequin Special Edition or Harlequin Heartwarming series and my 2 FREE gifts (gifts are worth about $10 retail). After receiving them, if I don't wish to receive any more books, I can return the shipping statement marked "cancel." If I don't cancel, I will receive 6 brand-new Harlequin Special Edition books every month and be billed just $5.49 each in the U.S. or $6.24 each in Canada, a savings of at least 12% off the cover price, or 4 brand-new Harlequin Heartwarming Larger-Print books every month and be billed just $6.24 each in the U.S. or $6.74 each in Canada, a savings of at least 19% off the cover price. It's quite a bargain! Shipping and handling is just 50¢ per book in the U.S. and $1.25 per book in Canada.* I understand that accepting the 2 free books and gifts places me under no obligation to buy anything. I can always return a shipment and cancel at any time by calling the number below. The free books and gifts are mine to keep no matter what I decide.

Choose one: ☐ **Harlequin Special Edition**
(235/335 HDN GRJV)

☐ **Harlequin Heartwarming Larger-Print**
(161/361 HDN GRJV)

Name (please print)

Address                                                                                    Apt. #

City                                        State/Province                          Zip/Postal Code

**Email:** Please check this box ☐ if you would like to receive newsletters and promotional emails from Harlequin Enterprises ULC and its affiliates. You can unsubscribe anytime.

Mail to the **Harlequin Reader Service:**
**IN U.S.A.:** P.O. Box 1341, Buffalo, NY 14240-8531
**IN CANADA:** P.O. Box 603, Fort Erie, Ontario L2A 5X3

**Want to try 2 free books from another series?** Call 1-800-873-8635 or visit www.ReaderService.com.

*Terms and prices subject to change without notice. Prices do not include sales taxes, which will be charged (if applicable) based on your state or country of residence. Canadian residents will be charged applicable taxes. Offer not valid in Quebec. This offer is limited to one order per household. Books received may not be as shown. Not valid for current subscribers to the Harlequin Special Edition or Harlequin Heartwarming series. All orders subject to approval. Credit or debit balances in a customer's account(s) may be offset by any other outstanding balance owed by or to the customer. Please allow 4 to 6 weeks for delivery. Offer available while quantities last.

**Your Privacy**—Your information is being collected by Harlequin Enterprises ULC, operating as Harlequin Reader Service. For a complete summary of the information we collect, how we use this information and to whom it is disclosed, please visit our privacy notice located at corporate.harlequin.com/privacy-notice. From time to time we may also exchange your personal information with reputable third parties. If you wish to opt out of this sharing of your personal information, please visit readerservice.com/consumerschoice or call 1-800-873-8635. **Notice to California Residents**—Under California law, you have specific rights to control and access your data. For more information on these rights and how to exercise them, visit corporate.harlequin.com/california-privacy.

HSEHW22R3

# HARLEQUIN
## PLUS

Try the best multimedia subscription service for romance readers like you!

---

## Read, Watch and Play.

Experience the easiest way to get the romance content you crave.

Start your **FREE TRIAL** at
<u>www.harlequinplus.com/freetrial</u>.